TO: DAD   MAY 18, 85

WITH
LOVE: Lisa

THE
SCOUT PATROL BOYS
IN THE FROZEN SOUTH

BY JACK WRIGHT

THE WORLD SYNDICATE PUBLISHING CO.
CLEVELAND, O.   NEW YORK, N. Y.

Printed in the United States of America
by
THE COMMERCIAL BOOKBINDING CO.
CLEVELAND, O.

THE SCOUT PATROL BOYS
IN THE FROZEN SOUTH

CHAPTER I

Headed South

"How are we making out, Uncle Dick?"

"First class, taking it all in all. Andy Clark assures me the big airship is in better condition than ever he knew it to be."

"And he surely ought to be a good judge, seeing that he put it through its paces for months, down in the frozen Southern seas around the Antarctic Pole. But he's never flown over the mighty snow-capped Andes, all the way through Columbia, Ecuador, Peru, and Chile to Cape Horn, or Tierra del Fuego, as we're meaning to do now— is that correct, Uncle Dick?"

"Absolutely so, Jim; but remember, Andy is a famous air pilot, who was given high praise, also several decorations, by the French Government, because of the number of enemy ships he sent down in flames during the World War. Since agreeing to take us down to the frozen seas, Andy has left no stone unturned in getting together all the maps and charts, as well as information covering this marvelous Andes country."

Jim Lawrence and his uncle, Richard Lawrence, the famous explorer, accompanied by Jim's scout brother, Phil Williams were on their way to undertake a search for Richard Lawrence's old comrade,

Professor Jules Chapman, a famous scientist who was unfortunately left to his fate when it became necessary for the main body of his luckless Museum expedition to board their vessel and leave the scene of their four months labors.

"For one I'm trusting Andy to carry us through in great shape; and Uncle, I too have been soaking in all the facts covering the mountainous country over which we figure to drive as fast as this speedy and modern cabin amphibian can take us, so I'm pretty well posted. Besides, you know I am a fair air pilot, so that in an emergency I could relieve Andy without going into a bad spin, and crashing."

"That goes without question, Jim. You proved it when you handled that unwieldy six passenger plane belonging to our eccentric Western cowboy friend, Slim Blair, and carried us all the way out to his plains ranch without any accident."

"Figure on dropping in on New Orleans by evening, do we?"

"That's the schedule, Jim; but there'll be no opportunity to give that quaint city the once over on this trip, since we are in more or less of a hurry to finish our great flight, and reach the limitless ice fields where our job is waiting for us. We must jump off tomorrow at dawn."

"I want to ask Andy a few questions now—matters that have cropped up since we took off this morning. Lucky we're well supplied with these wonderful ear-phones; with all this racket of whirling propellers, and both engines working at full speed, it would be mighty hard to carry on a conversation without yelling at the top of our poor strained voices."

"That's straight talk, Jim, and what is your patrol partner Phil Williams doing to amuse himself?"

At that the sturdy young fellow whose name was Jim Lawrence, laughed and nodded his head as he went on to say:

"For three hours steady now he's just sat there, gazing through your new binoculars, drinking in the thrilling checkerboard pictures "away down below-stairs," and trying to gain experience by figuring out what rivers and cities we pass over in our first leg of the new flight. And that'll be his occupation, besides getting meals as agreed on, day after day; and believe me, he's tickled to death in knowing he can hang on to those powerful marine glasses you bought just before the start."

"I've got a hunch," said Dick, nodding approvingly as he spoke, "that this trip will be of immense educational value to both of you patrol boys —all of us, in fact; for although I've explored many strange and dark corners of the world in my time, this will actually be my first experience amidst Polar seas."

Jim and Phil, although members in good standing in a scout troop of their native town, carried no emblems of their connection on their persons. They were wearing clothes that were prized for their ability to resist rough service, and aboard the airship they had the warmest possible garments for use when at high altitudes, or spending long nights amidst the endless ice floes and bergs of those mysterious and perilous southern seas.

So, too, they carried a number of guns along, for the chances were they might have to depend on them as a means for procuring food. No wonder then they were thrilled at the prospect of speedily seeing South America from a vantage point miles high; but the prospect of spending weeks, perhaps months amidst those unexplored regions close to the South Pole, was an incentive to many day-dreams calculated to make their boyish hearts beat high with anticipation of glorious adventures to come.

The ship was "doing herself proud," as Andy had taken occasion to remark more than a few times. He surely ought to know what the big plane could do in the way of making great speed, since he had been its pilot during all the time the baffled ex-pedition from Washington had swung around in far-stretched circles, bearing the eminent scientists hither and thither, as their plans demanded; and never once had it failed to meet up with his ex-pectations.

As was to be expected Uncle Dick's time while on the extended journey would be mostly taken up with studying the maps and directions he was carrying with him. Being a man who was particu-lar about having things condensed, and in their place, he had arranged matters so nicely as to be able to put his hands on anything required without losing even a precious second.

"If I have any faults or weaknesses," he often told his observing and admiring nephew, Jim, "and who has not; carelessness isn't in the list. I have found it a valuable asset to keep everything in systematic shape, for much valuable time is saved by so doing. Call me a crank for neatness if you will, but that has become a maxim with me; indeed, one of your most emphatic slogans is 'Be Prepared,' and it pleases me to note how you lads keep that in mind. It will grow upon you, too, as the years glide away, and you arrive at manhood."

Some time later, in the early afternoon in fact, Jim sat down besides his best pal, who had again returned to his favorite occupation of scrutinizing that section of the country over which they were passing.

"Where are we now, Phil?" he asked.

Phil laid a forefinger on the map he had open on his knees, and without any hesitation stated:

"I've figured it out that we're passing over the low mountain district on northeastern Georgia, and that Atlanta can't be so very far ahead."

"My opinion exactly, old partner," said Jim; "for I've got a mental picture fixed in my head, of the course Andy set for making Orleans."

"If you look over to the southwest," continued the observer, (as Phil had decided to call himself), feeling he must have *some* plausible reason for being among the crew of the wonderful ship; "you'll notice a heavy cloud that hugs the earth, even with the sun shining from an unclouded sky."

"H'm! smoke I take it," suggested Jim, at the same time casting his eyes so as to take in what his companion had just mentioned.

"Well, that would be Atlanta I'm guessing," continued Phil. "I've heard from Joe Kingdon, whose folks used to live in the Gate City of the South, that when there's no air stirring it's often so dark at ten in the morning motorists have to turn on their lights so as to avoid having trouble; and in spite of that precaution there are frequent collisions. Of course we don't expect to drop down on Candler Field, where so many airships gather, coming from every direction, some bound for Florida, others heading toward Mexico, or it may be the Northwest?"

"Not unless something makes it wise to have the plane serviced," Jim told him, he having put that same question to the pilot not ten minutes before. "We want to get to Orleans before dusk, have the gas supply built up, and then possibly head to cross the Mexican Gulf during the night, so saving time, which will be a valuable asset taken in all."

"Well, if we do that I reckon I can sleep in fits until morning comes around, and shows us how far we've traveled toward our next harbor at the Canal. By degrees I expect to get so used to being on a speeding airship at night I'll sleep just as sound as in my bed at home in old Martinsville."

"No question about that, Phil; it's like traveling in a Pullman sleeper—the first night out and you are restless, dozing parts of the time; but every night after that you seem to drop off to sleep without any trouble, to wake up hours later, and be surprised to realize how you're a couple of hundred miles further on your journey. Almost everybody goes through that experience, I imagine."

"We're getting closer to the smoke cloud, you notice, Jim, and it's beginning to thin out, so there must have been a breeze sprung up to carry it away. Yes, and through the glasses I believe I can catch glimpses of tall buildings, for Atlanta has a number of sky-scrapers I understand. Take a look and tell me if I'm right."

Ten minutes later and they were above the Georgia capital, Andy having obligingly dropped down from the lofty ceiling that had been followed for some hundreds of miles.

The black smoke cloud had also been kind enough to drift off to the southeast, so they had a fairly clear view of a city neither of the two patrol boys had ever seen before, and of which they had only read and heard. But shortly afterwards they lost sight of the city and were again heading in a direct line for New Orleans.

Whether they should stop overnight there, store their ship in a rented hangar on the field, and go to a hotel for the night; or else deem it best to continue their southern flight early in the night, must be determined later, as conditions chanced to face them.

Phil displayed a little disappointment at the possibility of not being able to give the Cresent City the "once over," now that he had the opportunity; and so wise Jim took occasion to enlighten him.

"You must always keep in mind the serious task Uncle Dick has taken on his hands, even to risking all our lives in carrying through the success of this undertaking. Then too, don't forget that at this very minute those three lost scientists, if still alive, may be beginning to despair of ever seeing their loved ones again, as their provisions keep on getting less and less, and the hope of being rescued grows dim. We've just got to subordinate everything else to making speed, without being too eager, and ruining it all by taking too great chances."

"I know that, Jim, and I'm sorry I showed a sign of regret," pleaded the repentant Phil, humbly enough. "Not for anything selfish on my part would I give Dick cause to wish he hadn't agreed to take me along. And really I'm now hoping we'll decide to cut across the gulf tonight, if the weather report turns out to be favorable for such a trip."

"And well said, shipmate," his chum told him, patting his shoulder approvingly. "We've pledged ourselves to carry on this big drive Uncle Dick so willingly took on his shoulders through loyalty to the comrade for whom he cherishes such affection; and on his account we're not going to let any side issue far less important draw us away from the main track."

"You just bet we wont, Jim, and my word for it you'll never see me looking disappointed again. I was merely interested in the queer sights I've read about in New Orleans—the famous French Market, the headquarters of those notorious old gulf pirates who lay in wait to capture treasure ships on the Spanish Main; the quaint cemeteries where the dead are placed in overground tombs because it is almost impossible to dig five feet down without coming to water, so near to sea-

level does the city lie; and lots of other things
that've taken a strange-hold on my imagination.
Some fine day later on maybe the chance may come
for me to set eyes on those things; and I'll always
feel better because I put them out of my mind
when duty called."

That sort of talk from scientific Phil made Jim
more than ever fond of the other. He sat there
for a short time making use of the magic glasses
in order to see at short range the character of the
country over which the giant air-ship was speeding; but it was so monotonous a spectacle that
Jim finally tired of looking, and went off to do
something he felt could better occupy his time.

Two hours later, with the sun about an hour
above the western horizon—that is, it would ap-
pear so from the surface of the earth a mile and
more beneath, though it could be plainly seen
from their lofty lookout for twice that length of
time—Phil announced that they must be approaching the city on the mighty Mississippi; for he was
able to locate Lake Ponchartrain, and could plainly
see a boundless body of water to the south, that
must necessarily be the Mexican Gulf.

When they could see New Orleans directly below them Andy circled to get his bearings, and
then proceeded to bring his charge down in a
perfect three-point landing on the extensive airport that did such credit to the air-minded people
of the far-famed Crescent City of Louisiana.

CHAPTER II

The Gulf Storm

First of all Dick meant to get the latest flying weather report, so they could make their decision concerning the next thing to do—stop over, or make a night flight further south, so as to gain that much time.

Andy told them he would stay by the plane, as he wanted to give things a look over, as well as have the ship serviced—with gas tanks filled again to their utmost capacity. The others could get their supper while in the city, and if they found time fetch him out a few fat sandwiches, also a bottle of ginger ale, of which it seemed he was abnormally fond.

After Dick had scanned the figures and probabilities for the next dozen hours, as given by the Government reports of flying conditions Uncle Dick looked very pleased. Jim surmised from this, knowing the wish for making speed that lay foremost in his Uncle's heart, that the probability was it meant going on, and making a night of it.

"We shall be on our way short of ten tonight," Dick announced.

"Good enough," said Phil quickly, "suits me okey, sir; and maybe now early in the morning we'll be dropping in on that big ditch at Panama."

"God willing that's what we hope to be doing, Phil; and," continued Uncle Dick, with some show of feeling, "I want you to know how glad I am both of you are just as eager to reach our far-away destination as I myself am. I felt certain I was making no mistake when I asked you to share the trip with me; you certainly are chips off the old block."

"Then the weather promises to be fair tonight, I take it, Uncle," Jim changed the subject.

"Practically so," came the reply; "though of course a passage such as crossing the wide Mexican Gulf should never be taken without extra precautions being observed. Andy tells me that at any time tricky shifting winds are liable to spring up, over that vast body of water; and more than one luckless aviator, lulled into carelessness by conditions surrounding him, paid the penalty for trusting to treacherous fair winds and deceiving skies; sudden squalls are apt to arise as if to catch a half napping pilot off his guard, and overwhelm him with disaster. But come, let's find a restaurant where we can have supper. After a good meal we'll get to the airport, and make ready for taking off once more."

Dick had been in New Orleans before, and was able, with little difficulty, to lead them to a famous restaurant in the French Quarter, which rejoiced in a liberal amount of patronage from tourists and natives. In passing a particularly evil looking corner he pointed into a dimly lighted former barroom, and told them:

"That's the identical place known in the old

days of this city as Headquarters for a piratical
gang that scorned the law of the land, and carried
on their *evil* work, snapping their fingers at all
efforts to bring them to justice, and the hangman's
rope."

"Whee! it makes your flesh creep just to picture
those dreadful days of old, for a fact," Phil was
saying; for while the others had spent their spare
time in filling their minds with facts and figures
calculated to assist in their dangerous quest, he
had followed his own bent, and got many a thrill
from reading accounts of those old filibusters and
pirates; which was why he shivered as he stared
into that evil looking barroom where those dash-
ing and lawless historical cutthroats were wont
to congregate, and plan many of their villainous
campaigns in search of treasure on the high seas.

They enjoyed their supper very much, since
only a light lunch had been eaten at noon; and all
of them had excellent appetites, sharpened by
their late passage through the upper starta of the
atmosphere; after which Dick got the waiter to
have several generous and tasty sandwiches made
up for Andy's private consumption.

They continued on their way, each of the boys
carrying a couple of bottles of ginger ale, Dick
holding on to the package of succulent sandwiches
for Andy.

In due time they turned up at the hanger where
they found the faithful pilot just finishing his
task of overlooking the engines and wings of his
charge. He had during their absence seen to re-
newing the gas and oil supply, the port having

facilities for supplying all necessities connected with life among the clouds.

"What's the answer, sir?" he remarked as they entered the big hanger temporarily sheltering their ship.

"Everything seems favorable for a night flight, Andy," Dick informed him, and not by the flicker of an eyelid did the veteran pilot show that the news affected him either way—take it or leave it was his rule of life, from which it was easy to decide Andy must be something of a fatalist, as many air pilots are, due to the fact of leading such a hazardous existence.

"And the ship is in tip-top shape to carry on, I assure you sir. If fortune favors us with a half-way decent night we should not be far away from Colon, or Panama, by dawn, I take it, sir."

"It would be a good sign if we could make Panama inside of twenty-four hours from our start this morning; few ships have made as fine a record, and I'll accept it as a good omen we are to be favored by Providence in our undertaking."

Their up-to-date ship was arranged to take off either from land or water, according to which was the more convenient, being furnished with both wheels, and illuminum pontoons that could be raised or lowered at a moment's notice. They had no difficulty in rising from the airport, the illumination being everything they could wish for; so in good time they were on the air road again, headed a few points from due south-west.

It was dark, as the moon would not rise until a little later, being close to its last quarter. Phil was sitting where he could lean over, and look down toward the unseen earth. By making use of the glasses he could manage to occasionally glimpse a speck of flickering light, which, with a stretch of imagination, he could well believe might come from some lone cabin.

He knew that this was a part of the Mississippi delta, often drowned out when the great river went on a rampage; and that those hardy or careless folks who continued to come back to their poor quarters after the riotous waters went down on each occasion, did so because they knew not where else to go; and no matter how humble it might be, home had its strong appeal.

Now even this fragmentary evidence of humanity vanished. Phil guessed the ship must have passed out over the body of sub-tropical water known as the Gulf of Mexico. He could not make certain of this fact by any effort on the part of his eyes; but by sniffing smartly, (for they were not at an unusual altitude) he fancied he could detect a saline odor in the night air that bespoke salt water.

When half an hour later the moon, shorn of some of her roundness, ventured to peep above the eastern horizon—though it was still as dark as pitch down below; Phil, found himself becoming a bit tired of straining his eyes, he started to yawn, which was a good indication he would be ready for his bunk before long.

When later on the silver moon was high enough in the partly cloudy sky to be shining on earth and water, Phil could make out the foam on the billows that seemed to be rolling shoreward, as though there might be quite some breeze close to the gulf's surface.

By degrees he yawned, and his head would drop only to be lifted again with a start, then to repeat the performance.

"Better drop out, and snatch some sleep, Phil," suggested Jim, who had been watching the other try to resist his drowsiness, and felt sorry.

"Huh! reckon I might as well, brother," agreed the sleepy-head, suiting his actions to the words.

He lost consciousness of passing events almost as soon as his head touched the pillow. The engines roared, and the twin propellers sang their shrill song, but all this racket seemed to have no effect on the tired boy.

He did not know how the hours went after that, so deep was his slumber. Some time later, after midnight it must have been, Phil suddenly aroused. The noise still continued, though it struck Phil in diminished volume, as though one of the motors was doing all the work.

He was shivering as if with cold, which certainly was not the case at the time he turned in. His hand while groping about came in contact with a heavy blanket, which some one must have thrown over him as he rested there, dead to the world. He could see a patch of sky from where he lay; and as the moonlight was very meagre he guessed it must have clouded up.

Phil sat up.

Somehow he became conscious of a queer feeling, as though the atmosphere was more or less rarified—he decided the pilot or his substitute Jim, taking a spell at the wheel, must have decided to climb to a higher ceiling for some good reason, that was the only explanation to account for the change in conditions.

As he had more than half expected would be the case he found Jim holding down the duties of working pilot, thus allowing Andy to secure some sleep, which he needed very much.

"Hey! what's this all mean, Jim?" he demanded, his head close to that of the other.

"We've been doing some pretty lofty climbing since you took to your bunk," the one at the controls told him, exhibiting no surprise at being addressed so suddenly with this demand.

"Clouded up, wind rose, and started to blow great guns—we had a confab, Andy, Uncle Dick, and myself, and as there was a chance of baffling currents of agitated air taking us unaware on either quarter, we decided the best thing we could do was to get to a higher plane, and ride the storm out, —which we did without any more discussion."

"How far up does the altitude instrument say we've come?" asked Phil.

"Something like three miles from the surface of the gulf. The wind is blowing up here too, but steadily. That wasn't the only reason we decided to get out of that mixup down below."

"What's happened, Jim?"

"A bit of bad news for us, Phil; but after all, while it may slow us up a bit, nothing serious happened. One of our twin motors took a sudden notion to go back on us, and that accounts for the diminuation of the racket we're making. Go back and get more sleep, Phil; there's really nothing to worry about, only we'll have to lay over when we get to Panama, while Andy and a couple of plane mechanics overhaul the engine, and put it to rights again."

"What time is it now?" Phil asked as if desirous of knowing it all before condescending to continue his slumber.

"Seven minutes after three, as near as I can figure, since we have to change our watches every day or so during the run down to Cape Horn."

"Gee whiz! did I sleep that long, while you fellows kept on deck and handled our big ship? Why, it won't be long now before the dawn will break; be sure and wake me up when the light starts to come in the East; I want to see what daybreak looks like three miles above the big pond down there. Tell me, was there any thunder and lightning with the storm you mentioned? I don't remember hearing the crashes."

"Only in the distance, and then spasmodically," Jim told him; "it was a queer old sort of a storm, mighty wind gusts and twisters with the lightning flashes brightening the entire sky."

Satisfied that there was no occasion for alarm, even though one engine was "on the blink," as Phil himself expressed it, in his boyish fashion, he returned to his cozy nest, and was speedily again lost to the world.

This time it was a hand that shook him, and Jim's voice rang in his ear shouting; for Phil did not wear his clumsy but useful earphone outfit as he wooed the goddess of sleep:

"Peep o' day, buddy; if you want to see the sunrise better hop out. Clouds have passed away and it's as clear as a bell overhead, with promise of a fine morning. Andy is at the controls, and we're slipping down the grade leisurely. It's possible you'll soon be able to make use of your glasses again, when light comes to the world below."

Accordingly Phil amused himself for the next half hour drinking in what to such an erthusiastic admirer of Nature was a most glorious sight, with the eastern heavens a mass of dazzling colors, amidst which presently the king of day thrust his smiling face, as if to welcome the pilgrims to this southern clime.

When the show was all over at that altitude, Phil could turn his attention to other things. He found that they were still passing high over the gulf, and at a short distance from a tropical shore, which he quickly decided must be a part of Central America, the vegetation seemed so dense, with jungles and all manner of palm and palmetto trees visible through his powerful binoculars.

And they were already heading toward the shore. Evidently Andy had decided to cut across country, soar above a range of mountains he could just manage to make out in the distance, and head for the strange city of Panama on the wonderful Canal that Uncle Sam had constructed on

the site of the one other engineers had made such
a failure of many years ago.

Hours later they came upon the canal with its
immense locks, and basins, and circled over the
city of Panama.

CHAPTER III

A Night Attack in Lawless Panama

Safely landed they first of all looked after their ship, just as the Arab Bedouin of the desert never fails to immediately pay attention to his faithful horse, before wasting any time on himself.

Andy Clark took this job on his hands, and soon had a co.. of airplane mechanics busily engaged under his directions, with a promise that the overhauling of the defective engine would likely be finished by evening. Uncle Dick hated very much to lose a precious day; but it could not be helped, and he felt himself fortunate it was nothing more serious.

"You are lucky, Phil," he told the other, who was going around with a grin decorating his face; "what's a day in your calendar of bounding youth when there's an interesting city to be visited? So make the most of it, lads, both of you, while the opportunity is here. I've been in Panama and Colon before so I'll just hang around the ship— somehow I just don't fancy some of the hangers-on you can see in squads, and they might mean trouble for our air flier. We'll just have to sleep aboard of her tonight, for protection; got to come to that soon, and, might as well get accustomed to our limited quarters."

Jim and Phil did a heap of roaming about all parts of the canal city, made up of all manner of odd people; for when the canal was in process of building the high wages paid tempted men of all climes to head for the isthmus; and many of them have remained in that torrid zone ever since, adding not at all to the lawful character of the places where they made their abode.

Several times it became the part of wisdom for the two American boys to change their location, before matters grew a bit too warm, for squads of these evil characters began to dog their footsteps, apparently sensing a rich opportunity to acquire dollars with little effort.

"I must confess," Phil was saying, with upturned nose some time later, as they decided to leave the city and spend all the balance of the day investigating the locks through which several big steam vessels were passing; "I reckon I'd hate to stick here in this hot and smelly place. If it's this bad now what must conditions be in the middle of the summer?"

They picked up considerable information concerning the canal locks, and how the costly land slides happened every now and then, mostly on account of the torrential rains that came in the wet season. Along about high noon the boys picked out a likely looking American restaurant, where they had a very good dinner, and tasted several dishes that were native.

After much more walking and riding they concluded at about half-past four they had had a sufficiency of Panama life, and should call it a day.

Arrived at the place where so much bustle had been going on around their ship, they were surprised as well as gratified to find everything calm, the air-carrier safely housed in a big hangar, and Uncle Dick having a quiet chat with the pilot.

"We'd better go to supper in detachments," the former was saying as the two weary lads came along with lagging feet; "for I reject all thought of leaving our precious means for continuing our important voyaging with any of those tough looking men in the offing. Come and see what has been accomplished, fellows, thanks to our efficient pilot, Andy Clark here."

"Looks bangup I'd say sir," Phil agreed, after a superficial survey, "p'raps it was lucky that if it *had* to come the accident to the motor happened while we could make a stop-over, and secure efficient assistance."

"Glad to hear you say that, Phil, it shows you're an optimist, always ready to make the most of a bad bargain," and Dick gave the other one of his brightest smiles, that made the recipient feel very proud.

As Dick and Andy had only managed to get a "snack" at noon they chose to be the first pair to go to "grub;" the boys gave them directions concerning how to reach the restaurant where they had made their midday meal, and which they proposed heading for again when they went out for supper.

The evening came with a brilliant sunset, that

painted the heavens so red it almost looked as though the old world was on fire. As Jim and his pal were coming back after they had partaken of a very good meal, it was beginning to grow dusk. Things were taking on a more sinister appearance by then, owing to the deceptive light— men whom they would have hardly noticed in the broad daylight had the look of sneaky prowlers, who given half a chance, would not hesitate to hold them up, and try to rob them of any money they carried.

With this in mind it was Jim's policy "safety first always," to keep a bright lookout, and refrain from passing through certain dingy passages which would appeal to loose characters as just the places for robbery.

His suspicions were redoubled when he saw several fellows running ahead as if to waylay them; to a Jim took the bull by the horns, crossed over glimpse, and policeman whom he chanced to guard.   k him on for a dollar as a body-
"I didn't quite
Dick later, "but like to do it," he explained to pride to bring us, I couldn't allow a little silly men. They seem into a nasty fist-fight with those
"You showed a d to be looking for trouble."
you did," his uncl lot of sagacity in doing what have to sacrifice l e assured him; "we sometimes such an important ooks for safety; and while on bad if we were del mission as ours, it would be too ities because you a yed several days by the author- of black eyes, and d Phil gave somebody a couple
besides," he added with a wide

grin, "there was a chance that either of you might have been seriously injured, and confined in the hospital for an unlimited period, which would compel the rest of us to leave you behind. All in all, I'd bet on the first thought."

As all of them were very tired it was deemed the part of wisdom to retire early. Even the noise of airships taking off, or making a landing, did not interfere with the sound sleep of Andy, Dick and Jim, but Phil had one of his wakeful fits, and for a long time just lay there in his berth, his mind a jumble of myriads of adventures, both those which had already happened, and those awaiting them when they got far down the Andes region.

When finally he dropped off it seemed as though only a few minutes had passed before he felt a hand shake him gently, and Jim's voice whispered in his ear the thrilling words:

"Mum's the word, Phil—it's Jim. There's a bit; I thing going on outside that I don'+ hear whispering and shuffling."   awake Phil whis-

"Gee whiz!" the suddenly wide- glad we brought pered, "Boarders ahoy, is it? I'm a fine chance to those guns along with us· here's lugs. Does Dick try them out on some Panama th know, and Andy too?"   t the sounds first,

"Yep, it was Andy who caugh n got me up the and nudged Uncle, who in tur im informed him, same way I'm doing for you," Jtrol, and whisper- still keeping his voice under con ing in his chum's ear.

"Great guns! this looks squally; what are we going to do to knock them galley-west?"

He slid off his cot, and crouched down, trying to see something in the opaque gloom; but without success. He did catch the suspicious sounds of men's gruff voices toned down to a soft refrain; also a fumbling about the already partly opened window that gave them fresh air.

Taken in all it was very thrilling, and Phil felt his blood grow hot as his fast-beating heart pumped it through his arteries at a double quick rate.

Immediately afterward he bumped into Dick and Andy Clark, crouching there, and waiting until the attack had come to such a pass that they would have something to aim at if they chose to let fly with their handy guns.

In whispers then they conferred, while in a huddle, and arranged to commence shouting in concert when the signal was given by Dick.

"Do you suppose they know we're all in here right now?" Phil asked in a low voice that trembled more or less, due to the vast excitement under which the boy was laboring.

"Possibly not," Dick told him, softly, "that would all depend on whether they saw a light inside this hangar earlier in the night. I don't just understand what they are after, unless they've got a silly notion we are rich Americans, whom they can rob of treasure. Then again I strongly suspect they've been doing a lot of drinking—you know as in Mexico, they make a liquor down here from the agave plant, called aguardiente, or mescal, that is strong enough to knock a horse out with. At any rate they seem bent on getting inside this plane hangar, and the window is really the only vulnerable point that I can discover."

"But we're just as bent on keeping them from doing that," Jim added, and Phil noticed there was not a sign of a quaver in his chum's even voice—the Lawrence boy was not in the habit of showing excitement under the most formidable pressure.

"This is becoming a regular nuisance," Dick declared in an irritable tone, "and we don't need to stand it much longer. Of course they're not going to get in, and that settles it. We've got to give the bunch a scare, and a rattling one at that; but boys, we don't want to shed a drop of blood, first because we haven't any really hard feelings against these misguided marauders; and secondly on account of our desire to get out of here at an early hour tomorrow morning. Get that?"

"Yes, sir," said Phil, and the others also joined in making it unanimous.

"Well, when I fire the first shot all of you start yelling bloody murder, and also let loose with your guns, aiming *above* their heads, not below. I warrant you that racket will be followed by a grand scamper; nor are they likely to come back for a second dose. Ready now, for we must be on the wing, headed for Columbia as our next stop-over, before tackling that mighty Andes chain. Here goes!"

With that Dick fired his gun—it was a double-barreled shotgun, so that he had yet another charge reserved. Instantly it seemed as if all Bedlam had broken loose—guns cracked and bellowed, voices were raised in a volley of shouts calculated to send the cold shivers down the backbones of the would-be house-breakers. Between times Jim could hear retreating footsteps and cries of alarm.

"Hold up, fellow," he bawled out; "they've beat it, and while the going was good. I reckon we'll not be bothered any more this night. Now if only all this racket hasn't attracted the notice of the Panama police force, who might give us trouble, we'll be lucky."

Possibly the gallant force was not at all anxious to mix in a fight with that wild gang of hoodlums, fearing later reprisals; or considered it just a little jamboree that did not concern them, at any rate they did not make an appearance on the scene. It was midnight, leaving the four Americans several hours in which to catch their "forty winks." At dawn there was a movement in that field hangar, and they soon had their big cabin plane swung out on the runway, ready for a take-off.

"Nothing left behind, boys?" demanded Dick, who himself supervised operations. "We can't afford to miss a single utensil, for there may be no chance to replace them later on down the coast-ways, or over the endless jungle and forests of the Amazon country. Okey then; so we go!"

It was so very early that there were few spectators present to see them take to the air; and those people offered not the slightest objection to the departure. Jim was half anticipating some sort of a hostile movement, possibly by members of the foraging gang of the previous night; but if any such were present they were held in leash by their fears of the American firearms.

Down the runway they started, gathering momentum as the big plane roared and shook, until rising like a condor on the wing they left Panama far behind.

CHAPTER IV

Over Amazon Forests

With the departure from Panama their dangerous flight changed its character—not until they reached Cape Horn would they find themselves speeding over the sea, most of the trip being taken up with negotiating a passage over mighty mountains, or at times the impenetrable jungles and forests of the Amazon region.

"On for Bogota!" Phil was saying to himself, hours later, as they sighted the land again near the boundary line between the republic of Panama and its former parent state, Columbia. "Gee whiz! even the fact that we're just going to step on South American land gives a fellow a nice thrill."

They were fortunate in not having met with any important trouble up to this point, the affair of the dry storm in the Gulf, and the encounter with that rough element of Panama's floating population not counting for much. But none of them dreamed this freedom from mishaps could last much longer.

It was a glorious spectacle when, having climbed to a lofty altitude in order to pass safely over the mountain ranges, they had a wide and rugged landscape spread before them like an enormous map.

Andy, supplemented by Uncle Dick, kept a direct course for the centrally located Columbian capital, hidden away up among the mountains of the State—the weather man was kind, and dealt out only favorable winds—both engines kept up their unceasing grind; and going thus almost a hundred-and-fifty miles per hour they were cheered late in the afternoon by the discovery through Phil's overworked glasses, of glimpses of a city that they were convinced must indeed be Bogota.

Such proved to be the case, and as the landing field turned out to be pretty up-to-date they met with no trouble in dropping safely down, after circling the field three times while diving lower.

How fortunate for the party that Uncle Dick could speak pretty good Spanish—this fact was of wonderful importance to them all their journey through the whole Southern hemisphere, and where it happened that Portuguese was spoken they had little difficulty of meeting on a common ground.

They were warmly received by the officials of the capital, who on learning the nature of their extended flight could not do too much to add to the comfort of these unexpected visitors.

However, Dick was compelled to decline a reception and dinner; he and his three mates were too tired and sleepy, and must needs conserve their strength to the utmost in order to carry through the onerous labor of meeting and overcoming the tremendous difficulties lying beyond.

They saw that their precious plane was safely housed, a guard being offered by the commandant, who could not do too much for these dauntless souls who had dropped down from the skies to honor the Columbian capital by their presence.

Conditions being still favorable they were off again in the morning, after the amphibian had been duly serviced, and the party given a delightful breakfast; so that their memories of Bogota would always be exceedingly pleasant.

They had been wise enough to ask questions, and gathered much information, that was apt to prove most valuable as they headed for Peru; and if given time that afternoon they planned to drop down to the low altitude of the headquarters of the mighty Amazon.

Again did good fortune attend their efforts, for before evening shadows gathered to usher in a dark and forbidding night they found themselves floating on a stream which Dick calculated must be one of the upper tributaries of the great Amazon.

Anchored in the middle of the deep stream they prepared to pass the night, regardless of hearing all manner of strange noises, from jabbering monkeys, fierce outcries from hungry, roaming jaguars, the splashing of crocodiles and manatees in the river; and kindred sounds without number, many of which they found difficult to identify.

"It's easy to see why Dick was so careful as to supply nettings of wire mesh for all the openings of our cabin," Phil was remarking, as he began to prepare their evening meal which was to be very simple, since it was not wise to attempt to have any sort of fire when the fumes of gasoline were present; "we'd be eaten alive by these hordes of mosquitoes only for that."

"Don't be too sanguine, Phil," chuckled Jim, "unless I miss my guess, if this fine breeze dies down later in the night, you'll find yourself fighting swarms of sandflies, punkies, or other minute pests that can come through even the finest of wire mesh. To secure any peace you'll have to wrap a towel around your head, and even then you will be constantly rubbing at your neck which will seem to be on fire."

"Yes," added Dick, frowning as if he did not contemplate the future with much satisfaction, "we'll know more about the many species of minute insects by the time we make Cape Horn, than any of you dreamed existed. Even as far south as the floating ice fields there are times when the explorer has to fight these pests. But we'll survive, I imagine, fellows, so don't grow discouraged."

It proved to be a night long remembered, and their sleep was so disturbed that red eyes were the rule when at last dawn arrived. They even ventured to go ashore to light a fire, and have their customary coffee with fried bacon and eggs; the eating of which gave them new vim. To find an open stretch of the river they were compelled to taxi for nearly a mile down the crooked stream; but in due time it was possible to get afloat once more, after which they speedily gained the desired altitude, and headed south.

They were of course now in Brazil, and beneath them lay the seemingly endless dense tropical

forests that were as a rule moist, and so insuffer-
ably hot, for they were very close to the equator.

All day long they continued speeding along in
a nearly direct line, keeping a high enough ceiling
to find the air refreshing, and looking forward
with more or less dread to having to spend another night on some river, where their experience
of the previous night might be duplicated.

How strange it was, Phil told himself many
times during that remarkable day, to be covering
hundreds of miles in one of the most up-to-date
flying contraptions as yet produced, and never
once be able to detect the presence of a living human being, or the faintest sign of a habitation,
however, primitive.

"It seems just like we might be the only folks
on the whole surface of the earth," he at one time
confided to Jim, with considerable awe.

Dick was consulting his maps, and bits of information he had acquired from many sources.
Toward the close of the day he gave his verdict
as follows:

"We've kept this wonderful speed up since our
start this morning, and have covered enough mile-
age to bring us close to the dividing line between
Brazil and Bolivia. It is of some importance that
we reach La Paz, the capital of Bolivia, in another
twenty-four hours, as our gas is getting low, and
we'd be in a terrible fix if it were exhausted, leaving us far away from any source of supply."

Again they settled down for the night on the
bosom of a rapid little river that Dick declared
must indeed be the Madre de Dios.

"It has all the characteristics of that stream, as described to me; and you can easily see its general course is due nor'east, for at the end of its run it joins the great Madiera, itself the chief tributary of the Amazon coming up from the flooded south. If this is true then we are tonight across the border, and in Bolivian territory."

"Bully," ejaculated the pleased Phil; "and if we're allowed to get any decent sleep tonight we'll be more'n lucky. I'd like to wet a line, and see if the fish in this stream are good enough to eat."

"Nothing to hinder, if the bugs let you make the try," Jim assured him. "To tell the truth I'm a bit fish hungry myself; and it would be a crying shame if we spent so many nights on these South American rivers, said to be crammed full of fine fish, and never once got a taste of them."

So Phil took courage, kept a length of netting handy so he might be able to fight the enemy off if attacked, and went about his self appointed task with such zeal and luck that presently he had accumulated quite a basket of several species of fish, from which Dick selected those he believed to be most edible.

They had to land in order to cook their supper. Jim, not liking the looks of the shore was careful to carry a rifle along with him, with which he stood guard while Phil cooked the meal, which was carried aboard the anchored amphibian when ready.

There was more or less of a repetition of the mysterious noises of the wilderness forest during the stretches of the night. At one time indeed, such

was the clamor and splashing close by that Jim
sat up, and kept his rifle ready, thinking some
water beast was trying to crawl aboard.

However, nothing serious happened, although
several times all of them felt a violent bump as
some huge object came in contact with the alum-
inum pontoons that sustained the plane so suc-
cessfully.

In the morning they made a meagre breakfast—
it was so decidedly close and hot they drank their
coffee cold from the thermos jug carried for just
such occasions. Again they had to do more or less
taxi work until finally, after half an hour had
been spent in the search, a straight stretch in the
zigzag course of the Madre de Dios was discovered,
long enough for their purpose, although they almost grazed the tops of the tall trees as they
climbed upward.

Looking forward with hope to making La Paz
before sundown, they little suspected what an experience lay ahead of them before their plans for
the arrival could be consummated.

Along about two in the afternoon clouds rolled
up, and distant thunder gave warning of the ad-
vent of a storm. Dick had been cautioned against
being caught at a low altitude by one of those
violent storms as are prevalent all through the
territory south of the Amazon. There was hardly
time for them to gain altitude that would place
them above those heavy storm clouds so rapidly
approaching, consequently the next best thing
would be for them to drop down on the river run-

ning north, and the general line of which they
had been following.

All of the sky voyagers breathed easier after
they made their forced landing on the river.

"Well, that was what I'd call a close shave," Phil
gave his opinion, and the others heartily agreed.
"Now let the elements kick up all the row they
please, we'll be okey—unless the lightning takes
a notion to give us a call, which I hope wont be
the case."

The storm was one of the wildest any of them
had ever experienced, and held the stage for such
a length of time that Dick decided it would be
folly to think of continuing their cruise that fag-
end of the day.

"We'll just make the best of it," he told his
comrades in his customary philosophical fashion,
"and get a fresh start in the morning. From all I
can figure La Paz is not over three hundred miles
away right now, in a southwestern direction; and
given two hours speeding we ought to cover that
distance. When we sight a peak that rises something close to twenty-two thousand feet, mapped
as Mt. Illilampu, we'll know we're close to our
destination, for the capital lies just south of that
sentinel."

Either they were getting used to the wild clamor
of the wilderness nights or else there did not happen to be so much racket; just the same they secured a very decent night's sleep, and awoke at
daybreak much refreshed and heartened. Dick
took his calculations as usual, and once they found
themselves afloat in the clear atmosphere far above

the dense forests, he was able to lay out the course
and they forged ahead on swift pinions.

Phil had grown weary of gazing down on the
same monotonous spectacle; the novelty that first
gripped him had grown stale; and now he looked
most of the time ahead, in hopes of glimpsing the
towering peak, welcome harbinger of a decent
breakfast in La Paz.

"I guess you never do miss the water till the
well runs dry," he consoled himself by saying;
"and I never knew cooked meals could be so fine
till I didn't get any for a long time. Now let's
see what my order's going to be once I tuck my
legs under a restaurant table."

In the delightful pastime of making his selection
of choice food (although he must have known it
could never be fulfilled at any eating place in the
Bolivian capital) Phil forgot to keep up his vigi-
lance as a lookout; so he had quite a thrill coming
to him on resuming his duty.

"Huh! glory be, what's this I'm seeing—looks
like a dim mountain peak backed up against the
sky-line ahead there. Hope it isn't what they call
just a *mirage*."

But Dick almost immediately made motions as
if to tell the others he had sighted a most welcome
vision, and that their goal was close by.

Such indeed proved to be the case. As they drew
near the Bolivian city they began to feel anxiety
concerning the fact of making a safe and sane
landing. It turned out that there was an airport
awaiting them, and although it was hardly in a
class with those they knew in the States, yet

Andy had no difficulty in bringing his weighty charge down so softly as the admiring Phil hastened to declare an egg would hardly be smashed by the contact with Mother Earth; though Jim had his doubts concerning the truth of that story.

It certainly did seem mighty fine to again feel solid earth under their feet, and to know they could if they so desired sleep in a *real* bed the coming night.

With Phil breakfast was the leading thought, though he did have the courtesy to hang around until Jim could keep him company into town, and what Phil in his high-flown fashion denominated "our groaning board."

As before, Dick set duty first—he would stand by Andy and make sure their aerial steed was serviced, before attending to his own wants.

Phil's enthusiasm had gone down a few points after eating his breakfast at a table in a restaurant —at least it was called such—in La Paz; these South Americans it seemed, liked rich and greasy foods which did not please the youngsters.

"Oh! I guess I could get accustomed to anything, if I kept digging away long enough," Phil told his pal; "but give me the good old U.S.A. grub."

CHAPTER V

The Limited Express

"Everything ready for a quick getaway in the morning, Uncle Dick?" Jim asked the other, as they prepared to pass the night in a Bolivian hotel.

"Nothing omitted, or forgotten that I know about," came the comforting answer. "It seems that Andy doesn't like the idea of spending a night in a bed, and plans to stick by his charge—says his bunk is as snug as anything he could ever wish for; you see Andy's knocked around so much his idea of comfort is a whole lot different from yours and mine. Well, possibly our ship will be entirely safe where we've stored her, and there'll be no trouble, such as we met with up in Panama; but I think Andy wants to make assurance doubly certain."

The other trio took chances at the hotel; there was never much said about their checkered experiences, but Andy grinned when he discovered his mates scratching at some portion of their anatomy every little while during the following morning, evidently in the belief that actions speak louder than words on many occasions.

The take-off was unattended by any accident, nor were there many spectators to watch them climb skyward. Doubtless the good people of La Paz were fond of their morning nap; then again the hour was really too early for their customary habits.

It was just as well, for the aerial voyagers disliked publicity, and tried to avoid it as much as they could.

"What's our next port of call, Commodore?" Phil was asking Dick as he adjusted his binoculars to suit his eyesight, ready to pick up his favorite occupation of watching the moving panorama far down on the earth as they sped swiftly along.

"If by that you mean what city will we strike next," he was informed; "our plans call for Buenos Aires, although at first we considered entering Chilian territory, and reaching Santiago. But as we are something like fifteen hundred miles out from the Argentine city, in a direct line southeast of here, it's likely we'll be compelled to put in another of those delightful nights, hugging some convenient river for a safe harbor, and only too glad to find such a place, but don't worry, my son; all this is getting us down to brass tacks— making us accustomed to standing *anything* that comes along; if men *will* take chances amidst the ice fields and floes of the Polar seas, they must expect all sorts of hard experiences."

"I get you, Dick, and believe me I'm almost in good trim already---couldn't possibly be anything more ragged than what we've already gone through."

"You think so, do you, Phil?" chuckled Dick with a twinkle in his eyes. "Well, you've another guess coming, I take it---live and learn."

"Gee; is that so?" Phil was heard saying, half

to himself; "p'raps after all I ought to harden up some more then. But it's all in the game."

As they proceeded reeling off the miles methodically the nature of the landscape over which they passed changed more than a little from what they had experienced further north. Instead of a perpetual and dense forest they met with open spots, where the ground was visible; small streams cut through all this, and occasionally Phil glimpsed a cluster of crude habitations; but the altitude at which they were flying at the time practically prevented him from being able to determine whether the ant-like objects he could see and knew to be human beings, were either dark-featured Argentine citizens or native Indians. Phil had no great interest in learning the answer to this puzzle, since he did not anticipate meeting any such inhabitants one way or another.

He did experience something of a thrill when suddenly a moving figure attracted his attention ---yes, it undoubtedly was some species of the cat tribe, perhaps a jaguar, or else an ocelot, leaping in pursuit of some small prey that was trying to seek safety in flight.

The monotomy was somewhat broken along about noon, when there came another storm that threatened to give them some trouble. But Andy, being an old and experienced pilot, saw he had an abundance of time to get well above the clouds, and as the prospect looked anything but bright for a forced landing he preferred the other alternative.

So cold did the atmosphere become that they had to don heavy coats in order to keep from shivering until their very teeth rattled in their jaws. The almost constant roll of thunder below them, and the brilliant flashes of electric fire darting from one cloud to another made it resemble some weird orchestra striking up with its heavy pieces.

If not dangerous at least all this was decidedly thrilling and spectacular. Neither Jim nor Phil had ever experienced what was now being given as if for their special benefit; there was something majestic about witnessing a wonderful storm from a gallery seat above the clouds a mile or more, that caught their imagination, and so long as it lasted they sat there with a sensation bordering on awe, as something worth while remembering.

Not until it had fully passed, with the hot beams of the lately eclipsed sun bearing down from a clear sky, did Andy feel it safe to descend from his lofty altitude, and continue their passage much closer to the earth.

Again they looked ahead as the afternoon waned, seeking some harbor on some friendly lake or river; because night flying was absolutely tabooed, unless perilous conditions demanded it as the choice between twin evils.

Several times Phil drew Dick's attention to a pleasing prospect on a line with their passage, only to have it rejected after the "once over." It seemed as though Phil's judgment in such matters did not wholly satisfy the veteran pilot, who relied on his own long experience, instead of simply pleasing and inviting appearances.

But it became a different matter when later on Dick himself discovered just the spot for them to drop down on. Besides, it was close on night, which had a way of following the passing of the sun so suddenly that it was apt to upset the plans of those not accustomed to such queer proceedings.

It was really a little jewel of a lake, partly hidden by the surrounding forests. After Andy had carried out his customary investigation by making three turns around the water, he saw no reason why they should not take possession forthwith.

True, it seemed an utterly uninhabited section of territory; but that was a whole lot in their favor; solitudes where no human being had his habitation were more of a sanctuary than otherwise; they had more to dread from the scum of cities than with regard to wild animals, or reptiles.

Besides, they wanted to risk going ashore, and do some cooking. Opportunities for such enjoyment would be "scarce as hen's teeth," Phil offered in defense of his proposition.

In the end it carried the day, opposition fading out as in imagination the others already caught the delightful whiff of boiling coffee, backed up by slices of home smoked and tender ham sending up an aroma that just *could* not be resisted.

It had been pitch dark for some little time when the cook called his three mates to supper. They had found some sort of make-believe seats in the way of stones rolled up from the border of the miniature lake, and as everybody was tremendously hungry the supper vanished in much less time than it had taken Phil to do the cooking.

It might be noticed that the same extra degree of "safety first" had apparently appealed to each one in turn, judging from the fact that their entire armament was displayed, in case any sudden necessity arose for holding off a sudden attack from savage men, or beasts, objecting to having their private hunting preserves invaded by these strangers.

After they had dined sumptuously, (as Andy remarked), they just took things easy, and lay around, Dick and Andy smoking their pipes with the satisfaction of tired men resting after the day's labor was done.

The conversation was general, and naturally mostly connected with the daring mission calling them to this southern clime. There were certain facts that would undoubtedly have a strong bearing on success or failure; while nothing may have been mentioned about them before, plainly Dick had borne them in his mind continually; he being the head and brains of the whole enterprise.

But it was Jim who brought up the subject as they sat or lay around the crackling campfire so many thousands of miles distant from their homeland. "I'm doing a whole lot of worrying, Uncle Dick," he ventured, frankly, taking advantage of a break in the rapid-fire conversation; "about whether the arrangements you made by wire with the steamer captain, whose outfit took the Museum's expedition into the frozen seas, and later returned in such a hurry, were understood enough to cause him to keep waiting for us at that rendezvous for some time after the date you arranged."

Dick nodded, and smiled, as though he had little fears concerning such a possibility; then taking the stem of his pipe from between his strong teeth he proceeded to remove the last fear from Jim's mind.

"I have kept from mentioning that up to now, because I felt Captain Barbour would stick to his post for a reasonable time after the day set had passed by. He had those express orders from authorities at Headquarters, and is a broad-minded man, as well as an expert along the line of knowledge concerning the perils of polar exploration."

"His orders as I understand it, were to put aboard everything in the way of stores that would duplicate those taken originally. It was put that way because the officials did not know with certainty that any of us knew enough about such things, and would neglect some things on which success or failure might depend — is that so, Uncle?"

"You hit the nail on the head, Jim; as for myself I have only a theoretical knowledge of these things, and am depending on Andy here for guidance. But let no doubt enter your minds, any of you, concerning the fact of the *White Bear,* as the steamer is named, being on hand when we arrive, even if we should be a week late; all that has been positively taken care of."

Jim said no more on the subject that had been

giving him considerable anxiety. He knew when Dick gave such strong assurance there would not be any grievous blunder made endangering the success of their expensive rescue mission.

"As this idea of mine," Phil remarked later with a little pride in his voice, "to make land, and enjoy what I call a bully supper has turned out all to the good, I'm hoping we can do something along the same line for breakfast. Fact is, I've been fairly itching to give you all a feast of genuine flapjacks, like our patrol pal, Teeny Morse used to turn out for the whole gang every day, that time we spent a week up my granddad's hunting lodge in the Adirondacks. How about it, Uncle Dick?"

"Count me in, if you can get up extra early, in order not to detain us about making out start. We ought to get *somewhere* before many hours, or there may be a mess of trouble over a lack of gas."

"So ordered, so done," Phil added, a satisfied look on his face, for by now he was becoming a bit proud of his hitherto unknown culinary abilities.

"In all probability," Dick further remarked, "while on the subject, I rather imagine this may be our last stop in the wilds for a short time. We are now close to a settled part of Argentine, and within an hour after we jump off in the morning I expect we'll sight the railroad leading down the Parana river into Buenos Aires."

This plan was carried out without a hitch. Breakfast was eaten ashore, and Phil's first attempt at making flapjacks turned out fairly well, though he realized he had much to learn before he could call himself as accomplished in that line as fat little Teeny, who could even toss them up in the air when partly cooked, without a miss. Phil decided not to attempt any of the "frills" as yet; he wanted to do a little practicing in private before "making an exhibition of himself."

They took off without any trouble. Dick and Andy had held a council of war, and settled upon their course after reaching the proper altitude. Soon Phil was delighted to see evidences of civilization continually, and almost took a fit when he first discovered a real railroad train speeding along at what might be forty miles an hour, but which resembled a snail's pace when inspected from such a great height.

Santa Fe, and then Parana were passed, with Phil keeping his eyes fairly glued to his binoculars. Then later on they shot past Rosario, quite an extensive city, also on the growing river that at its mouth was known as the Plata.

"Next Buenos Aires!" he exultantly shouted above the roar surrounding them, at the same time waving his hand, as though too overcome by delight to say much more; "everybody go ashore—to get filled up, along with the ship."

"Two hundred miles more or less still ahead old scout!" yelled Jim, as none of them save Andy wore their handy ear phones; and he only discarded his harness when off duty.

"Nothing at all," Phil whooped, "to such a racer as ours has proved to be. And tonight we'll be able to go to a hotel for the very last time, since once we leave this city behind we'll have to rough it right along."

So on they roared along their way, keeping up their fast pace steadily. An hour passed, and soon in the distance Phil could detect a vast blot of smoke against the sky, and from this reckoned they must surely be nearing their destination, a wonder city, like unto a second New York or Chicago, where the latest luxuries known to civilization would be in common use.

CHAPTER VI

From the Equator to Cape Horn

It suited Dick's purposes and plans for them to place the amphibian in a garage where it would be safe from molestation, and take his two young allies with him to a fine hotel. As Phil had mentioned it was bound to be their last chance to taste the sweets of civilization; and he could sympathize with their desire to spend a brief time amidst the things they were accustomed to enjoying when at home.

Just as might be expected faithful Andy absolutely declined to accompany them, much preferring to stay at the fine aviation field, and take pot luck so far as bed and meals went; he did not much doubt that with money aplenty in his pockets he could get along without "starving to death."

During the last hours of the afternoon the boys managed to get a hasty glimpse of the Wonder City, while Dick did some telegraphing, and called for such mail as might have been forwarded to the South American metropolis. He was not visiting Buenos Aires for the first time he assured them, and even put his charges wise to certain sights they must see during their brief stay; the intention being to skip off early as usual, and tackle the last lap of the great trip down to the vicinity of Cape Horn, the always stormy tip of South America.

They retired early, hoping to get a sound sleep so, as to put them in good shape for a continuance of their flight. Once they boarded the stout little steamer selected for rough work among ice floes that might close in and do some squeezing, they would have things easy until again boarding their airship to start searching for the *cache* supposed to be the haven of the missing scientists—if still in the land of the living.

There existed the usual clamor of all great cities up to the hour of midnight; but accustomed to the roar of a speeding plane this did not annoy the lads one particle.

Their alarm clock awoke them at daylight, and presently they went down to the hotel lobby to there await the coming of Uncle Dick, as agreed upon.

"No use getting a morning paper," observed Jim, chuckling, "since neither of us can read Spanish well enough to make head or tail of the news. Dick can do all that for us, and tell what big things are happening throughout the world in these last few days. There he comes right now, on the dot, as usual. Seems like the Lawrences as a family always can be depended not to oversleep."

They had made arrangements for having an early breakfast, and a few minutes after Dick joined the boys all of them were seated at a table in a small coffee-room, and had given their orders.

Jim glanced several times at his uncle's face. It struck him something must be worrying Dick, for he frowned every little while. and shook his head impatiently, as though to thus chase away trouble. Noticing Jim's mute questioning he presently explained.

"It's really nothing, Jim; once in a while I get one of these fits, probably from some dream, although I never did believe in premonitions of coming evil. But it was very vivid—a fire bell or whistles may have sounded while I slept, and had some sort of effect on my imagination—I dreamed there was a big fire, and that, well, we lost our gallant and necessary ship — silly, of course. Forget it, and tell me how you like that omelet on your plate—mine is excellent, and Phil here looks as though he's heading for a second helping."

Settling their bill at the desk they ordered a taxi, had their bags tossed aboard, and then started for the airport outside the city limits.

They kept up a running fire of conversation as they sped along—Phil frequently called their attention to numerous things that looked strange to his Northern eyes; he was bubbling over with youthful spirit.

"Well, there's the aviation field, with a ship just coming in from the east, p'raps from Montevideo, or even Rio Janiero! Sounds mighty strange to be mentioning those cities, and to know we are so close to both."

Uncle Dick suddenly gave utterance to an exclamation, and Jim, glancing, saw how he had half arisen from his seat and appeared to be staring fixedly in a certain direction.

"Upon my soul there *was* a fire last night, and as I live it was out at the airport in the bargain!" Jim heard him say in dismay.

The thrilling words gave him a cold chill; then came Phil crying:

"Look, would you, the big hangar—*our* hangar, it's gone, and the ashes they're still smoking and smouldering! Gee whiz! after all we've gone through to have this happen, and spoil everything. Oh; shucks! it can't be so; I must be dreaming things again!"

He started to digging his knuckles into his strained eyes, as though striving to clear his distorted vision. But Jim by now had realized it was alas! all too true. His face went as white as chalk.

A great crowd made a circle around the charred remnants of the unfortunate garage, an old building, because most of the others seemed constructed of metal, and were thus fireproof.

Even as they all jumped out on the outer fringes of the gaping, chattering, crowd they heard a shout.

"It's Andy," cried Dick, "thank Heavens, at least he has escaped injury. Now we'll know the worst that can have happened."

"Look, he's grinning, fellows!" whooped the observant Phil, with exultation dominant in his tones. "Maybe now it isn't so very bad after all."

"What's happened, Andy?" demanded Dick, clutching the outstretched hand of the air pilot as he came limping up; "You're lame, you must have been up against it pretty hard. The ship—?"

Andy thereupon pointed to some object a short

distance away, and they saw the familiar cabin, wings and fusilage of the amphiban.

"Tell me, has she been badly injured—need repairs that may keep us marooned here?" Dick thrust at the other.

A shake of the head in the negative, and then Andy crying out:

"Not a flame touched her—never even raised a blister on the fusilage! We got her out, and trundled over there in good time; and they've set a guard to watch that no one does her any harm. Lucky again we are, Mr. Lawrence, sir; you must have been born under a favorable star I'd say."

"Tell us about it, Andy—what caused the fire, and to this old garage in particular. We have no enemies in the wide world, but it could hardly have been an accident. And why are you limping, were you injured?"

"Oh! that's next to nothing," Andy assured the anxious Dick; "to be sure I did my best to get the fire under control, but several more buildings caught and went up in smoke before the Fire Department arrived, and stopped the spread of the flames. Gasoline aplenty out here to help a conflagration along, once the spark is applied. Managed to trip over something I was fool enough not to notice, and got a bit of a sprain. I'll rub my ankle with some liniment as soon as we're ready to jump off, and it'll be okey in a jiffy."

"Is the cargo of gas and other things aboard Andy?" asked the other, eagerly.

"Sure thing boss; had it all tucked away early last night, and slept in my regular bunk until I was wakened by shouts, and saw flashes of light. Then I got busy—some men belonging to the port gave me a helping hand and we managed to trundle the ship out of danger before a spark touched off her big load of liquid fuel. If you are ready now, sir, we can be starting off."

"Can't be jumping too soon to please me, I'm telling you, Andy; if we hung around too long we might not be allowed to make clear, for the authorities would hold us to question, and harry us. Yes, let's get moving right away, boys!"

There was a tense little interval—only a few minutes at most, Phil fairly tumbled into place, for he could not remove his staring eyes from those uniformed police mixed up in the still gathering crowd. He feared lest he should see a hurried move being made in their direction, hearing at the same time loud voices demanding peremptorily in Spanish that they delay their departure.

But nothing occurred, so when Dick had given the propeller a few whirls, and Andy promptly moved the stick, the thing was done. Phil breathed naturally once more as he saw Dick climb aboard.

No one appeared to notice their departure. Away they sped down the runway, which was in excellent shape, gaining momentum with every second, and finally when Andy shifted his hand grip they left the ground, ascending gracefully like a great bird of the upper air currents.

And so they left Buenos Aires, with but a hazy idea after all concerning its leading characteristics; but then there was a method in their madness, since any delay so as to have an investigation take place, in order to learn who had set the old garage on fire, and just why—would have spelled complete disaster to their mission.

"Well, after all it might have been a whole lot worse," Phil was confiding to Jim, after they had watched the picture until the great metropolis faded completely away.

"I should say so," came the emphatic response; "I nearly suffocated during those last few minutes — seemed like hours to my imagination. It would have been terrible if they'd have stopped us on some ground or other, but here we are, free to keep on our way, no matter if a dozen buildings went up in smoke last night. Goodbye Buenos Aires, if it were evening I'd say 'buenos noches' to you—goodnight!"

Having intently followed their course all the way down to this point, Phil spent a whole hour or more in studying the map and trying to figure where they went from there.

Feeling that Jim was fully acquainted with his uncle's plan of campaign he finally turned to that fellow voyager, and propounded a number of leading questions that elicited more or less important information.

If all went well they were likely to make the balance of the journey in the space of two more full days. That was counting on decent weather, for should it turn stormy—as might occur when so near turbulent Cape Horn, the windiest point of all capes in the wide world—of course they were bound for delay. But so long as no serious disaster came along Phil on his part meant to utter no

complaint—not that it made any difference what-
soever, since he was no king of the south winds,
to make them obey his will, or die down at his
command—no Joshua to cause the sun to stand
still over Gideon's Heights, until his army could
put the opposing Philistines to flight and defeat.

It had begun to grow somewhat monotonous,
this dropping down and spending nights in soli-
tude; but Phil never whimpered in the slightest.
At least this time they were tempted to make a
genuine landing, the nature of the terrain seeming
favorable to the eye of their pilot, likewise Dick.
The wheels touched solid ground—there were a
few little jumps, and also bumps—then the winged
airship came to a full stop.

Fresh water was found close by, and they were
able to make a cooking fire in a hole amidst the
stunted trees, which fact pleased Andy and Dick,
who were a bit uncertain as to what manner of
human beings inhabited this lonely strip of territory once known as Patagonia, before Chile and
the Argentine divided it between them all the way
down to the island known still as Terra del
Fuego.

If any trouble arose during this very last night
on their long journey over the entire stretch of
South America, it would indeed be "just too bad,"
Phil confided to his pal, as he busied himself in
getting some supper for the crowd. Fortune, however, was still kind, and nothing came along to
give them cause for anxiety; so again in the morning they started on the last lap of the adventurous
trip.

CHAPTER VII

Southern Seas at Last

"Say, tell me, did any of you folks hear something in the middle of the night that sounded like we were camping in the neighborhood of a regular menagerie of wild animals?"

Phil asked this question just before they clambered aboard the big amphibian in the morning, after finishing their breakfast.

Jim looked quizzically at the speaker.

"Are you in dead earnest, Phil, or do you mean that for a joke?" he asked.

"Really and truly, Jim, I either *did* hear the wildest screeching in the near distance; or else I had a nightmare, and dreamed it."

"I reckon it was a dream, then; seeing that I've known you to do some queer things in your sleep."

"You're wrong this time then, Nephew," observed Dick, smilingly.

"Oh!" exclaimed Phil, turning toward the speaker appealingly; "then you heard it too, Uncle Dick? That relieves me, I was afraid I was having delusions—imagination you might call it. And what did you make it out to be, sir? Do they have such beasts as *tigers* down in this stretch of South America?"

"To tell the truth, Phil, it's got me guessing try-

ing to place it. If we were up in the northern sector of the Continent, and I heard that awful
screech, I'd set it down for a jaguar; but down
here I'm not so certain."

"Did it bother you any, Uncle?" queried Jim.

"Not for any great length of time," came the
frank reply. "To be sure I lay awake for as much
as ten minutes, listening to learn if the beast was
coming any closer; yes, and instinctively my hand
reached out until I clutched my shotgun; but that
was the extent of my interest in the affair."

"It didn't come again, you mean?" asked Jim.

"Only in a modified way, as though the animal
might be a half mile off, and heading to the west.
So, since I was satisfied there was no danger of our
camp being attacked I dozed off once more."

Phil heaved a big sigh.

"Huh! d'ye know I felt kind of disappointed
when the beast sheered off; because I'd have really
liked to see what he looked like. I'm not a big-
game hunter, but I did think we'd have a few thrilling adventures with jaguars and other creatures
when covering the whole length and breadth of
South America."

"As for me," added Dick, shamelessly, "I'm just
as well pleased that we didn't run foul of such
ferocious wild beasts. That must have been wholly
because our voyaging was all done far up in the
skies, where they don't have such jungle terrors.
There was another thing we fortunately escaped."

"What was that, sir?" asked Phil.

"Vultures—big hawks, and feathered creatures,

that are to be found all along the Andes Mountains from Columbia down into Chile."

Phil showed more than an ordinary amount of wonder at that remark on the part of Uncle Dick.

"Gee whiz! what did we have to fear from that sort of flying thing," he exclaimed, getting ready to climb aboard their waiting craft.

"Well, to tell you the truth I never had any experience myself with condors or other giant birds; but I've talked with air pilots who have; and it gave me the chills just to hear them tell how such birds attacked their planes savagely. Of course there was little danger of the pilot being struck by the angry birds; but if a wing, or a spinning propeller happened to get mixed up with the giant bird, it would send them down in a tail spin, and no one might ever know their fate."

Phil looked relieved.

"I'm glad I didn't know that before," he frankly admitted; "I certainly wouldn't have felt so comfortable."

"I had a wary eye on them just the same," said Dick; "and if there seemed to be any chance that one of the flock would head in our direction, Andy was ready to do some tall hopping about to discourage an assault. All aboard now—here goes for Cape Horn—and the frozen South Seas!"

The propeller started whirling, Dick climbed aboard, and they were quickly speeding along the level ground, which had of course been earlier carefully surveyed by the sagacious pilot, who believed in that slogan of "Safety First."

The day wore away, with the big cabin bus

steadfastly pushing forward, and the motors keeping in excellent condition. That pleased both men, who realized better than their more youthful companions might, the seriousness of trusting their lives and fortunes, with no means for making repairs short of thousands of miles.

With the coming of afternoon Phil began to display unusual interest in his chosen vocation of Observer—he would lean forward and strain his vision in the endeavor to discover something that would indicate they might be approaching their goal. Dick had given the others a few pointers that doubtless he had picked up, either from his extensive reading, or else in conversation with Andy, who had been at this place on a previous occasion, and never forgot locations.

It was just as well he did this, for otherwise they must have found considerable difficulty in reaching the small community where they expected to find the steam vessel—waiting their coming.

Finally Phil clutched the arm of Uncle Dick, and bawled in his ear:

"I say, Uncle, would you mind taking a look—dead ahead? I seem to see something that makes me think we've arrived okey?"

Accordingly Dick accepted the binoculars and took a sweeping survey.

"Good boy, Phil;" he in turn shouted; "I can glimpse the ocean away over there, and Cape Horn just can't be very far away. Yes, and that tower is just what Andy assured me would be our first indication we'd arrived at our goal. I'd call this the most wonderful event of all my life—we have voyaged over the entire length of the continent and hit this small focal point without any wandering and searching for it."

"Everybody cheer," cried the exultant Jim, who believed their safe arrival must be a good omen covering the success of their hazardous mission of mercy.

They joined him in lusty almost frenzied whoops, with Phil swinging his arms in true cowboy style, a trick he had learned when out on the plains at the cattle ranch. What if the constant roar of both hard working engines and attendant noises did render their combined effort a bit weak and insignificant, the shouts at least freed their abounding enthusiasm and did them good.

Not long afterward Phil sighted a stumpy looking stoutly built steamer tied up at a rude dock, which he immediately guessed must be the one they expected to go aboard if everything was ready for their voyage to the region of the frozen seas, where their search must begin.

So they managed to drop down close by, the water being smooth enough to allow such a maneuvre. There was a jutting point of rocky shore protecting the tiny bay from the billows that were unceasingly pounding mightily on the outer side of the natural bulwark.

Their coming created a great bustle, considering the smallness of the settlement so far, far beyond the last fringe of civilization. Men—and a few women and children came running from every direction to greet the coming of the big plane—

a boat put out to take them ashore, leaving their aerial transport anchored in the bight; and after the racket and din of the engines was silenced, deafened though the travelers might be for a moment, they could hear some of the commingled shouts.

Even aboard the tied-up steamer there were seamen leaning over the rail gesticulating and chattering like magpies; evidently they were more or less pleased that their tiresome period of waiting was near an end, and the venturesome dash into the unknown polar seas begun.

One of the first to greet them as they landed was a heavyset, nautical looking man with whom Andy eagerly shook hands, and then introduced as Captain Barbour, skipper of the ice breaker *White Bear*, a vessel from the Far North, impressed into this service for the use of the Museum's late disastrous expedition.

Dick sized him up as just the man for such work—self-reliant, agreeable in his nature and master of his profession—a man whose crew would look upon him with utmost approval, and for whom they felt proud to work their hands to the bone, when strenuous situations had to be met and conquered.

It was found that they could take off without any considerable delay, after the amphibian had been safely placed on the deck ready for contact with icy waters.

Dick did not mean to give the word to start until he had found abundant opportunity to go over the whole list, and make sure not a single thing was lacking—plenty gas in the tanks, provisions, means for keeping warm in the region where icebergs abounded, and so on down to the most insignificant details, for no one could tell when an emergency might arise calling for the least of the articles on the list.

"A splendid record of efficiency, Captain," he told the skipper, when this tally business had been carried through; "never a thing lacking; and I shall always wonder how you managed to accomplish it so cleverly, down in this lonely, God-forsaken strip of land, with that heavy sea bucking up against those rocks eternally—never quiet they say for an hour—just marvelous, and believe me I'm mighty glad we're going to serve under such a stickler for duty, sir."

"How about getting off, Mr. Lawrence?" asked the other, looking highly complimented by what the scientist had just remarked, for he had conceived a great admiration for Dick, just as the other had in his case for the skipper.

"We are a whole lot tired, and unsteady on our feet," replied Dick wearily, "so perhaps it would be better to wait another day."

Both Jim and Phil felt a little relief when they heard Dick's decision; yes, they were tired, after being cramped in their positions aboard the cabin cruiser for so many days; and besides, the thought of striking out from this very last point of land, and heading into the unknown, was a bit awesome. Many days were likely to pass without their having a chance to set foot on *terra firma* again—nothing but floating field ice around them every minute of the time.

They watched while the crew managed to get the heavy amphibian aboard by the skillful use of stout block and tackle, fitted for just such a special purpose. This was finally accomplished, and the plane properly secured on deck, so that in case of heavy weather it might not be washed overboard, and lost. It was coming dark when this matter had been carried through, and shortly afterwards they were summoned to the saloon for supper.

Everything pleased Phil, who had been secretly yearning for a different brand of food from that served aboard the amphibian.

"This tickles me a heap," he mentioned to his pal, as they sent out for a second helping of the rice pudding completing the tasty supper the man cook had served. "With that fine *chef* along no danger of our going hungry on this trip, or getting sick on my cooking."

Jim grinned, and nodded his head. Under the skin all boys are pretty much alike, and appeasing the pangs of acute hunger is generally a universal failing with the breed.

They were shown to their cabins which proved to have comfortable berths, in fact, they were so inviting they decided to make use of them at once.

CHAPTER VIII

Among the Ice Packs

At peep of dawn they were all up and dressed, expecting that the start would be made without any more delay.

They had been breasting the heavy billows of the open sea for almost an hour, with the last speck of land in the misty distance, when they were called to breakfast.

"Somehow I just don't feel half as hungry as I pictured I'd be," admitted Phil, a bit woefully. He was looking "white about the gills," as he himself would have called it. "S'pose it's this up-and-down motion of the tub making me sea sick?"

"Might be that way with us both," agreed Jim; "I'm none too frisky myself. I was hardly expecting anything like this, after we'd been aboard a big plane so long."

However, in a few days the boys lost that squeamish feeling and their appetites increased to such an extent they wanted to eat five times a day.

The boys soon found themselves deeply interested in the passage of the squat steamer through those vast billows that seemed to be perpetually rushing up to mountainous peaks, having their white foamy tops cut off sharply by the fierce wind that kept blowing.

They spent much of their time, when they got their "sea-legs" in studying the compass, watching the helmsman handle his wheel, and using the glasses in hopes of sighting the first signs of floating ice.

In due time this became a continual sight; in every quarter there loomed up enormous fields of it, through which their stout little steamer pushed its steady way, at times battered more or less; but with no ill effect, thanks to the unceasing watch kept for dangerous signs.

It was on the fourth day that Phil came in hot haste to where Jim, bundled up in a heavy sweater, and pea jacket, was reading some magazine he had brought along with him from home. Phil showed signs of much excitement, Jim noticed, looking up from the printed page.

"What's happened now?" he asked, casually, not so given to emotion as the other; "see another whale, or is it porpoises, this time?"

The waves were far less severe now, as though they had gotten beyond the confines of those furious winds that gave Cape Horn its sinister reputation.

"First iceberg we've run across!" Phil told him, proudly, as though he deemed it a personal triumph in his being the discoverer. "Here, sit up and take a good look. Glistens in the sunshine like silver, and sure makes a dandy picture. I mean to snap it with my camera when we come closer."

Jim looked though the glasses and admired, though displaying little of the enthusiasm of his chum.

"They'll get to be pretty common after a while," he remarked, as if ready to resume his reading. "Fact is, we'll suffer from fears that we'll get trapped among a host of smashing big bergs, and be in danger of having our boat crushed like an eggshell."

"Well, anyway I'm going to grab my camera, and snap her off while the fever still burns high," with which remark the ardent camerman hurried away to the cabin to secure his outfit.

Jim was quite right when he said the bergs would become more or less common presently; day by day as they forged ahead, often butting up against head seas and winds that held them back considerably, they sighted more and more of the detached masses of floating ice, until shortly they could not glance in any quarter of the compass with seeing a serried mass marked sharply against the horizon.

Of course their peril grew accordingly, so that it affected progress. To go at reduced speed during clear nights was the best they could hope for, because to jam up against those immense towering bergs would be to risk having a hole knocked in their bow; or it might be the shock of the collision would detach a part of the threatening berg so that tons and tons of ice must fall with terrific effect upon the deck of the sturdy little steamer.

Frequently Andy carefully looked over his charge, the big amphibian, making doubly sure everything was in complete order. Jim could understand how the pilot felt the great responsibility resting upon his shoulders, and that kept him "on his toes" all the time; if the lost trio of scientists were finally located, and rescued from the fate that threatened them, much of the credit would lie at the door of Andy Clark.

One afternoon quite a storm struck them, throwing the small vessel up in the air as though she might be a cork in comparison with the tremendous power of the storm-tossed mounting billows. Phil began to feel a queer sensation at the pit of his stomach, not unlike what he went through during the early part of the cruise; but this time it was brought about by *fear,* acting on the sensitive nerves of the stomach.

"Don't be ashamed because of that," Jim told him, at the same time trying to bolster up his own sinking courage; "why, even old salts often feel that way when grappling with such a twister of a storm as this seems to be—Uncle Dick told me so just ten minutes ago." All of them were a bit worried, for those thunderous billows looked as though they were about to utterly overwhelm the dauntless stub-nosed ice-breaker as they rushed pell-mell onward.

But there stood Captain Barbour, grim of face, and with unflinching mien, pitting all his knowledge of things nautical against the fury of the stormy blasts; and winning out too, in the end. So eventually the gale left them, and went whirling off to leeward with many a surly growl and scream from wind and waves, twin elements of woe to those who "go down to the sea in ships" from times of antiquity.

After that the weather favored them, though the

ice peril grew greater with each passing twenty-four hours. Captain Barbour knew his job, and was now beginning to hope for a sight of some odd formation, marking a stretch of ice-covered land, at which he had kept his ship while the previous company had sent out both its seaplanes in quest of information of scientific value.

At noon word went around the vessel that their goal was in sight three points off the port quarter, showing how they had come all these hundreds of miles almost in true course—"fine seamanship," Dick called it, as he shook hands with the smiling skipper.

"Well, it begins to look like business," Phil was remarking, as he disturbed Jim, this time writing up his log, and thrilled him with the important news.

"I'm glad of it," replied the other; "it's bound to be a hard nut to crack, and the sooner we get started the sooner we'll learn whether we're in time, or not!"

He put away his little log-book, with a wistful expression on his face, as though he might be saying "I wonder now what sort of an entry I'll be making next on those pages—will it be a song of triumph or otherwise—yes, I wonder."

Much was fated to take place before the entries could be resumed; for the most intricate and baffling part of their undertaking now faced Dick and his two youthful pals.

It was rather an interesting sight, their coming upon the very spot at which Captain Barbour and his gallant blunt-nosed little steamer had laid up while those ambitious scientific gentlemen were scouring the entire vicinity for hundreds of miles in their amphibian cruisers of the air, bent on ferreting out some of the mysteries of the frozen south, up near the Pole that had so long defied previous attempts to solve them.

So, too, did the air pilot, Andy Clark look sober; no doubt he was picturing the buoyant faces of the three who so blithely set out from that identical rendezvous, to make their way afoot with a sledge during the absence of both planes on different important errands, their main object being to seek the distant *cache,* and secure valuable papers and reports that had been left there for the time being.

"Not a thing been touched since we quit in such a hurry," he remarked to the other three, after the *White Bear* had come to anchor close to where the ice-covered land lay.

Dick could from the manner of his saying those words so disconsolately understand how Andy must have been indulging in secret hopes they would find those they sought holding the fort at the anchorage, having in some fashion managed to make their way back from their quest, dreadfully alarmed of course to find no trace of steamer or comrades, and thus deserted in the midst of that bleak forbidding region of eternal ice.

"Perhaps it is just as well they didn't attempt to reach here," Dick remarked, more to comfort the grieving Andy than for any other reason. "You mean that here they would not have such a supply of food and fresh water as at the big *cache,* where much had been left some time previously?" asked Phil.

"You said it, my boy," Dick told him, amiably.

"Besides," Andy added, slowly and sorrowfully, "something may have happened to keep them from ever making a start—one of the three could have had an accident, broken a leg perhaps, and his faithful mates would not abandon him to his fate, even though they all eventually shared it."

"That explanation had occurred to me also," added Dick. "Well, here we are on deck, and bound to learn the truth, whether sad or joyful. Let us all hope it will be the latter, and that the anxious troubled home folks of those gallant fellows may yet be blessed with their company after these long days and weeks, even though I fear it will have to be a near-miracle if they are saved."

Preparations were started without delay. It was too late in the day to dream of setting forth, with the darkness so near. The days would be short enough, no matter what their length, and each night they must face the problem of carrying on as best they might, either on the ice fields, or, if an opening came handy, then on the water, with possibilities of peril all around them.

In the morning they set to work. The weighty amphibian was lowered from the vessel's deck, as ample provision had been made for accomplishing such a thing on the previous voyage of the *White Bear*.

Dick had his list in hand, and checked off each and every item as it was placed aboard their aerial cruiser. It was possible to carry an abundance

of food, blankets and heavy clothing, the main
cause for trouble lay in the line of drinking water,
and tanks of gasoline.

"From all I can learn," Dick commented to Jim,
who was standing at his side as the loading was
being carried to a finish, "there was quite a quan-
tity of gas stored at the *Cache,* those who were
there not wishing to bring it back—such is one of
the reasons for making a *cache* at any time—as a
storehouse for extra supplies that can be recov-
ered if the necessity arises; if not they can be left
where they lie, and some future expedition may
find them a god-send.

"It is possible," Dick went on to say, as he pock-
eted his finished list, "our friends could exist all
these weeks and months, if they stuck to the camp
where the *cache* lay. My chief anxiety is that
sooner or later they may have been influenced to
start back to the steamer, and got lost in some bliz-
zard that wiped out all their landmarks, if I may
so designate things where there is no land."

The time had now come for them to take off and
try out the plan that had been mapped with such
infinite pains and consultations.

Phil managed to keep from showing the nervous
condition of his mind as the critical moment arrived. When he shook hands with Captain Barbour the other could not help noticing his hand
was as cold as ice, though the grip he gave was
bordering on being frenzied. He knew what was
in the boy's mind, and could sympathize with him
fully.

"See you later, then, Phil," he hastened to say,

with a cheery smile. "We hope, every man on this boat, that you will find them alive, and be able to bring them back aboard your plane. Take care of yourselves, fellows; and run no unnecessary risks, for the weather is treacherous in this forsaken ice country. Goodbye, and God bless you all."

They took their accustomed places, and Andy prepared to start one of the engines. There was plenty of water ahead, with little floating ice, so the start could be made without danger of fouling their landing gear, or the useful pontoons.

Phil sat and looked back at the squat steamer, with the row of friendly faces lining the rail, each accompanied by a violently waving hand. Then came the opening r---, and the flying boat commenced to push ahead, the pace increasing as they left the anchorage, until presently they were ascending into the air spaces,

CHAPTER IX

Denizens of the Polar Deeps

"I hope we find those poor chaps alive," Phil remarked.

"Something tells me that is going to be the case," Jim said, in his vigorous way; "we didn't cruise down the whole length of South America, to have our fine plans dashed in the end. No, we're going to get results for our labor, you can bet on that; and go back home almost bursting with a satisfied feeling of having done our duty, and won out."

Phil brightened up vastly after he ceased looking back. There seemed to be something miraculous about the mere turning his attention toward the region where lay their goal, to bring about a reaction in his feelings, and presently he was laughing heartily over some incident that Jim told him, by way of his ear phones.

It was not as clear as could have been wished; but then Andy, who surely ought to know the vagaries of this Antarctic climate, assured them such was mostly the case, a misty haze frequently gathering to partly obscure the vision.

To be sure they could get the better of any such adverse state of the weather by climbing to a higher ceiling; but the only trouble in doing so was the fact that they were likely to stray away from the course marked out for their guidance.

There was really nothing for either Jim or his pal to do, save look around at the remarkable spectacle presented to their unaccustomed sight. As for Dick and the air pilot, they had to keep their minds on a score of matters, lest there be a slip apt to prove disastrous. Once they lost their bearings their task would prove doubly difficult.

"Seems like this is going to be monotonous scenery," Phil was saying through his phones as Jim sank down beside him. "Ice everywhere, and not the slightest sign of a green thing whichever way you look."

"You're right, Phil, and one thing certain, if ever we're lucky enough to get back to Martinsville, we'll never again complain because the summer sun has sort of dried things up a little. At its worst old Martinsville is a thousand times ahead of this frosty region. "But then you never do miss the water till the well runs dry."

"Andy keeps on a direct line, I notice," pursued Phil.

"As close as possible," assented Jim; "you see, the man who made that little chart for Dick knew what he was about; and if only we can keep following that by the aid of a compass, and the shrewdness of our leaders, we'll bring up at the *cache* —sooner or later. We're liable to miss our goal because of the mist that shrouds everything; in that case there would be nothing left for us to do but comb the whole region, until we glimpse the flag they were given to set up for the sake of any other crowd that might come along years later, and be in need of supplies."

"I'd say that was a pretty big job, taken in all," suggested the other, giving a swinging glance half way around the horizon; "why, it's worse right now than it was ten minutes ago; and if this keeps on we'll feel like we're hunting a needle in a haystack."

"When it gets that bad, Phil I happened to know what we're bound to do—drop right down on a strip of this same ice, and wait for the visibility to get better."

"Well, that strikes me as the only way out; and we can pass the time by eating our lunch. Oh! Jim!"

"What now?" demanded the other.

"White bear!" exclaimed Phil, more or less agitated it seemed.

"Don't tell me we're in sight of our steamer again, and have been making a complete circuit?" cried the other, aghast at the idea.

"Shucks! No, the first real Polar bear of the trip!" and Phil pointed off to the windward.

"I can see him now, old scout; and he's just as you say—a big fellow, too. There, he's scuttling off heading for that open water. I reckon the big racket we're making frightened him."

"Wow! what a splash that was, Jim, watch his head pop up. He's as curious as anything to know what it all means. Great sight, eh?"

"Oh! it'll be as common as dirt before long," Jim assured him. "And if I'm not mistaken over in that other direction some animals are lying on the ice close to that dark stretch of open water."

"Just what are they, maybe they're seals, though they look to immense for those swimmers—what d'ye think, Jim?"

"Sea elephants, or walrus, I'd say," came the ready answer; "through my glasses I can see the sun glinting from their shiny ivory tusks, that sea hunters value so much. There, they've taken fright too, at our racket, and are making ready to dive out of sight."

The fog grew rapidly worse, and before long Andy was heading on a decided slant for a vast ice-floe, over which they had been passing for ten minutes.

"Going to drop down, and wait for clearer weather, I guess," Phil was saying.

"Time we did so," Jim remarked calmly; "for it's impossible to see with any certainty a few hundred rods away. We might pass within a quarter of a mile without seeing any floating flag. Slow but sure is our best hold right now."

The landing, if such it might be termed, was effected without much of a jar, and they all stepped out to stretch, more from habit than because they felt cramped, since they had been aboard such a comparatively brief time.

"How far did we come from the steamer, Jim?" inquired Phil a little later, as the two sauntered about on the immense floe, while Andy looked over the plane.

"I happened to take a look a few minutes before we started dropping, and it was some eighty miles as the crow flies."

"Not so far providing you had decent ground under you," observed the other, speculatively; "but with such stuff to slide over, and make the going more strenuous it was kind of nervy for those three men to start out, dragging their sledge after them."

Dick and Andy called to the boys and they all compared ideas. There could be little doubt but that right then they must be somewhere close to their goal. Consequently they must be very careful how they went on planning to comb every rod of ice first.

Phil later on supplied the ingredients for the first lunch, and thus their growing hunger was appeased; egg sandwiches proved very acceptable, and the *chef* was flattered with compliments concerning his ability to concoct tasty tidbits.

The afternoon gradually wore away, and it became evident that they would presently be starting their first lonely night upon the limitless ice packs. It was anything but a delightful prospect; with poor Phil wondering what would happen if, during the period of darkness, the wind arose, and the ice began to show alarming cracks as though about to break up.

It was all right if this occurred during the daylight when they could see to make a runway out of the ice, or else get the amphibian into open water, from which it would be easy to make an ascent.

"I don't think I'll get a wink of sleep tonight," Phil confided to his pal, as he started to set out a second meal while day light still remained, since their means of lighting the interior of the cabin were rather meagre and old-fashioned; they used an oil lamp; some candles, and several electric hand-torches, the last to be held back for an emergency.

Jim smiled to himself—Phil was a queer duck, continually changing his mind—one minute confident, the next uncertain as the winds of the Antartic Circle, about which he had heard such severe reports.

"But he's a true pal, and that nobody can deny," was Jim's conclusion, just as it had always been before.

They partook of their supper, and joked as they ate, as if there could not be the slightest reason for thinking any evil hovered over their heads. When the night folded its curtains about them, Phil found it was not so bad after all. Why, it did not look anything like he had pictured it might. It wasn't pitchblack, thanks to that coat of ice surrounding them in every direction, and, which spread for miles and miles far beyond the range of the most powerful binoculars.

"Well, I hadn't thought it would be like this," Phil observed, as he sat on the edge of his bunk, and looked out of the window so close by. "It's just like twilight at home, when you can see things at a little distance, yet can't tell whether a black object is a stump, or a man bending over; but which in the end turns out to be your neighbor's milk cow, cropping the grass. Not bad at all, so here goes for a good sound sleep. 'Wake me early

Mother dear, for — tomorrow'll be the first of May.' "

So saying Phil turned in.

Yet after all, despite the brave front he had shown to Jim, when Phil slept at all it was fitfully. All manner of queer sounds came to him magnified of course by the harrowed state of his feelings—there were moanings galore, also a certain swaying movement under the big amphibian, as though that ice blanket might be protesting against carrying such a load, and indulging in all sorts of threatenings as to what it would do if this sort of thing kept up much longer.

Suddenly, at two o'clock, a sudden shock made the stranded plane shake violently. Of course everybody came tumbling from their bunks, wide-awake on the instant, Dick, reaching for his pet rifle that he had placed close at hand, did not show any signs that bordered on panic, a fact that encouraged poor Phil very much, for such confidence was certainly contagious.

"Was—it—an earthquake?" Phil blurted out before he gave himself a chance for a second thought.

"Well, hardly that of all things, out here on this ice pack, hundreds of miles south of the nearest firm land," Jim told him, being quite in the dark himself as to what could have happened to them. "Something seemed to butt up against the plane, and even moved it a foot or more, though we did block the wheels of the landing gear. How about it, Uncle Dick?"

"You've covered the ground, Jim," came the reply, as Dick proceeded to replace his handy gun, convinced apparently that he would have no need for such a weapon. "Andy, I saw you staring out the window just as I tumbled out of my bunk—glimpse anything queer?"

"Why yes, I sure did, sir," the pilot quickly answered, grinning; "even as I rolled out I heard a lot of shuffling sounds; then I saw some kind of movement out there on the ice. Couldn't make it out, for the mist had settled down worse than ever—looked sort of *bulky,* and it wasn't alone."

"A bunch of them, you mean, Andy?"

"Just that, Mr. Lawrence, and shuffling away from the stranded plane like they'd had some sort of shock."

"H'm! that settles it, I imagine," concluded Dick, chuckling. "Walrus beyond the shadow of a doubt —sportive old chaps with whiskers, having a gambol on the ice, same as lambs would in a green pasture up North. One happened to knock his head against our fusilage, and come near upsetting us, that's all. Now get back in your bunks everybody, and finish your nap."

"But I thought they only came out on the ice near some fissure—safety first, you know—so they could duck under if anything alarmed them," remarked Phil, still apprehensive, it seemed.

"So they do, as far as I know," Jim told him.

"But there wasn't a break in the ice within a mile of us when we were last able to see?" continued the anxious one.

"One may have come since we had our supper," Jim assured him; "common thing Andy told me a while back—they spring a leak, and make some sort of a grand shove, then quit, and seal it up again."

"Well, then I guess we can finish our sleep in our bunks instead of the icy waters. Me for some sleep," and Phil got all set for a good sleep at last.

CHAPTER X

Phil Causes Some Excitement

When morning found the party in their unique ice camp it did not afford them much satisfaction, for the weather conditions had only changed for the worse. The strange mist continued to hug the ice pack as though it had settled down for a lengthy stay.

Phil snorted his disgust on making this disappointing discovery.

"Gee whiz! and is *this* the boasted Polar climate I've read so much about in books and magazines written by famous Arctic explorers—we could beat it all hollow in Martinsville, and not half try."

"This is only one specimen," Dick told him; "you'll probably see all kinds of changeable weather."

Andy tells me it's probably as clear as a bell above this fog right now; and when a breeze springs the mist will blow away in a jiffy. Breakfast ought to be our leading thought just now; what are you going to give us."

That started Phil off on a subject which took his thoughts away from the gruesome weather that gripped them, and promised to interfere with their search, just when they were apparently close to the lost *cache*.

They had a camp cooking-stove, made of sheet-iron with them, but dared not attempt to make use of the same aboard the plane, since the odor of gasoline was so strong it would probably result in an explosion.

But there was nothing to hinder him from utilizing the efficient apparatus if he took it some little distance away. Dick saw him carrying it out of the cabin, and grinned at realizing they would after all be allowed something hot and tasty for the morning meal.

"Take it to windward, Phil!" he called out; "less danger of the gas fumes being carried to the fire—go a bit further, and it will be just okey. That's the ticket; now get busy, we're as hungry as timber wolves. I'll help so we can get started as soon as the weather clears."

Fortified for anything after a good meal they sat around to await the pleasure of the weather man. Along about nine Jim gleefully announced that he was certain he felt a whiff of air strike his cheek.

"Coming from the nor-east in the bargain," he added, after briefly studying the mess of vapor overhead, to see signs of movement there. "I don't know a thing about the weather down here, but where I live and do my camping that would mean a lot."

Ere long even Phil could see the fog was on the move, and minute by minute the morning breeze grew in vigor until finally they had a gleam of sunshine dazzle their eager eyes.

"Looks promising," Jim observed, pleased to know his prediction was to be fulfilled.

"Time to get ready for a start," Dick in turn was saying, himself more or less delighted over the chance to make a forward move.

He had been studying his little chart, and making certain pencil marks on it; just why the boys would not be long in learning.

By the time everything had been cleaned up, and they went aboard the amphibian, the sun was shining brilliantly from an unclouded sky, and a delightful breeze was blowing steadily.

Andy had been looking over the ice so as to avoid anything that might give them too many rough jolts. He had his course laid out, and felt no fears of not being able to make it. What satisfaction it gave Phil to find the big cabin plane again climbing in spirals to a level that would best serve their purpose; he was even thrilled with the amazing view afforded, now that the atmosphere was so clear, and free from mist.

Looking about him with his glasses Phil could see several bunches of sea creatures, walrus, and seals with even three white bears shuffling along, in search of an opening where they might obtain fish for breakfast.

Dick was seated beside the pilot, so he could confer with Andy as occasion arose. Jim understood the tactics to be employed in the prosecution of their search; they would have to cover the ground by flying up and down. All through the day this must be kept up, great care being taken to keep an even distance between their numerous passages from east to west. If after a hard day's work they had gained no reward, then on the following morning it must be all done over again, only this time from north to south.

Both boys kept constantly on the lookout, using their glasses diligently in an effort to locate some object that might resemble a tattered flag, whipping in the breeze. Again and again they would have a glimmer of hope, but it invariably turned out to be deceptive, much to their disgust and bitter disappointment.

The day was frittered away in this apparently useless scouring of the vast ice pack; but they only had their efforts for their pains, since nothing had been accomplished when along toward evening they discussed the idea of giving it up and making another camp where the field offered best results.

"You do the picking, Andy" Dick advised, having perfect confidence in the ability of the experienced pilot to make no mistake.

There was little trouble in selecting the site of their second night camp, since the ice looked very much the same everywhere. Accordingly they descended, not without feeling some disappointment, so keyed up had they become over the success or failure of their great mission.

On this occasion the sky remained clear, no sign of mist appearing, Phil seemed to be keeping unusually quiet while getting supper, a fact that excited the curiosity of his chum, who knew him like a book.

"Now I wonder what's in his mind," Jim was saying to himself, eyeing the other suspiciously; "when Phil acts like that he's always got some crazy scheme rambling through his mind."

But as nothing was said by the other Jim forgot his suspicions. Dick and Andy later on became engaged in a discussion of what plan should be brought into play on the following day, and it proved so interesting that Jim sat there drinking in every word.

"We've combed this sector thoroughly," Dick was saying, finally, "and made sure that *cache* can't have escaped our search, consequently we've just got to change our base in the morning, and set out to cover a fresh field. The only question is in which direction shall we work next—south, east, north, or west?"

They were in an earnest discussion, each giving his reason for thinking one or another quarter would give the best chance for success, when suddenly a sound came that instantly brought the whole three to their feet.

"That was the smash of a rifle!" exclaimed Dick, excitedly, for him.

"No question about it," added the astounded pilot, looking as though he could hardly believe his ears.

"Can we be close to the *cache?*" Jim advanced, in his bewilderment, "that shot may have been fired by one of the three lost scientists?"

"Where's Phil?" suddenly demanded Dick, as if for the first time taking note of the fact that the boy was not in the cabin.

"And that shot—seems to me there was something familiar in the report." added Andy, beginning to see light; "I've fired that rifle too many times in the years I've owned it not to be more or less familiar with the way she speaks. I do believe Phil's taken a silly notion to go hunting to break this dreadful monotony."

Jim was aghast at the idea.

"He must be out of his mind to try such a thing;" he burst out; "why, what sort of game could he expect to bag down here—at night-time too?"

"Possibly he happened to note that some seals or walrus were lying on the ice not so far away, just as we came down; and he's been stalking them. Come, we've got to start out and find the lad before any danger overtakes him. Those whiskered walrus bulls are apt to charge him if one has been wounded; and if it's bear he's run across he'd find himself in hot quarters right away. But there's been no second shot, which is a relief."

Hardly had Dick said those last words when there came another sharp report, followed by a third in quick succession.

Dick hastily clutched his double-barreled scattergun, loaded with buckshot shells; while Andy in turn snatched up a hatch that lay conveniently at hand; then both hastened to reach the ice outside.

Jim was at their heels, his heart pounding against his ribs like a triphammer. All he could lay hands on was a long-bladed bread-knife that Phil used in his kitchen work, and which made a weapon capable of doing more or less damage when properly handled.

Once outside they found that everything had become silent, though Jim imagined he could detect some sound that came on the soft night breeze from a point toward the southeast, which was the quarter from whence those shots had emanated. He was not at all certain, but it sounded to him like the mumbling noise some wounded sea monster might make when expiring.

"This way!" Dick shouted, starting off without a second's delay, with the other pair trailing at his flying heels.

They had not covered a hundred paces when Jim felt sure he could see some dark object on the ice. With his heart up in his throat, half choking him, he pushed on, with his knife ready to take an active part in any sort of scrimmage on the carpet.

The dusky object changed its color by degrees, and Jim saw it turning partly to white. Why, it must be a Polar bear after all; and there was no sign of life about it.

"Hello! there fellows," called out a well known voice, as there was a movement alongside the bear; "yep, I got him, okey, that's right! And some size in the bargain, believe *me*."

"Phil, are you hurt?" bellowed the excited Jim, as he staggered along quite overcome by all this excitement.

"I'm fine, never even a scratch," came the reassuring answer in boyish triumph. "That last shot knocked him silly; and this is a great old gun of yours, Andy, I want to tell you; shoots like an elephant rifle."

They came up to discover Phil sitting on the body of a big Polar bear that had evidently just ceased to breathe; if he had thought of it in time no doubt the rash boy would have struck the usual triumphant attitude, with one foot resting on the carcase of his fallen victim.

"Phil, you shouldn't have done this," said Dick, secretly tickled, but deeming it his duty to assume a stern attitude which he did not feel. "You've taken big chances, and foolishly at that; besides, you've given the rest of us quite a scare. Still, I'm glad you got what you've been yearning to secure ever since we glimpsed that first white bear some days ago."

"But then," replied the other unconcernedly, "I didn't start out with the idea of coming on a bear, Uncle Dick. I saw some seals on the ice, and meant to get one; perhaps this chap was after 'em too, with a supper in view, and crossed my path, which was bad for him, I'll say."

CHAPTER XI

The Smoke Signal

"Now that you've got your bear, Phil" ventured Jim, "what are you going to do with him?"

"Nothing tonight," said Dick, before the other could reply. "We'll have to drag the carcase up close to the ship, and leave it there. Chances are no animal will come around to disturb things, unless it's his mate wondering what's detained papa so long from his family. In the morning, Phil, if you get up extra early, Andy here and myself may help you take his hide off; you will probably wish to keep that as a souvenir of your exploit."

Dick kept his word after the coming of dawn; and so the reckless Phil was going to carry back a memento of the trip that would make the eyes of his boy friends in the home town grow round with wonder and admiration.

Jim had been given such a severe shock that he lay awake for a long time, visioning all sorts of dreadful things that might have overtaken the ambitious hunter of the ice fields near the South Polar circle.

At least the day had opened favorably for their purpose. A clear light blue sky hung overhead, strangely near, Jim thought; the visability, too, seemed fairly decent, and somehow his hopes ranged upwards once more. How fine it would be if the coming of another night should find them at the goal of their long voyaging by airship and steam vessel, with their finding the lost scientists alive and well.

Once again they soared aloft and commenced those back and forth flights ten miles to the west, and then a swing to the east then they would repeat the maneuvre back to a spot on a line with their start.

Twice Phil gave utterance to a sudden movement that startled Jim, but in both cases it proved to be a false alarm, and nothing came of it.

Dick himself had been casting frequent and rather anxious glances toward the south, as though he did not like what he saw there.

Jim noticed there were clouds gathering toward the south, which slowly but surely were coming their way. Nothing extraordinary about that fact, Jim concluded; but then his uncle was an experienced weather observer, being naturally gifted that way, as some outdoor men are; and he must see something to arouse concern about the character of those clouds and the way they continued to shoulder their way higher and higher, as the minutes dragged along, "wouldn't it be a shame," Jim was telling himself, "if we struck another of those Polar storms, and had to take to a ceiling far above the clouds as before. Such a thing would break up all our carefully laid plans."

Dick was talking to the pilot through his ear phone. Jim watched and thought he could note a shade of annoyance on Andy's face. Yes, and he also saw him give several quick glances toward the south, as if gauging the meaning of those threatening clouds.

More talk continued, but Jim was unable to guess what arrangement had been effected should the mounting peril actually burst upon them. He figured it would be impossible for them to drop down on the sea of ice, since the storm might prove to be of a violent character, such as would cause the field to break up, and they must be caught in a dreadful trap.

Then it was that Phil came into the picture again, having been strangely silent for quite some time. He nudged Jim in the ribs, and when that worthy turned his head he found the other grinning excitedly and pointing to the west.

"Look there will you, Jim," was what he said, "there's something queer that way—looks like a pillar of black smoke rising up; though what that could come from beats me, for Dick and Andy both told me there wasn't a single esquimau or any other kind of being that walks on two legs, within five hundred miles of here, except those lads aboard our steamer."

Jim was not listening to what the other said, for he found himself too much thrilled by what he saw through his glass which he had focused upon the object of Phil's discovery.

"It—is—smoke!" he declared, gaspingly; "such smoke as would come from burning blubber. Shake Dick's arm, and hand him your glasses, Phil."

Dick took the binoculars Phil thrust into his

hands, and leveled them in the quarter the boy's quivering finger was pointing to. Jim saw that he was instantly deeply concerned, for he glued his eyes fast to the instrument, and seemed to fairly devour the picture of that mysterious black smoke cloud rising in a direct column far away to the west.

Then came spoken words to the pilot, who also gave a hurried look while Dick grasped the controls. The excitement spread like magic; there was a sudden swing, and the ship was headed directly toward the west, and the beckoning smoke signal.

'Say, you don't think it could be coming from the stack on our steamer, do you?" Phil was asking Jim.

"Well, hardly, Phil, since that vessel's about a hundred miles as the crow flies, from here. It's something better than that, strikes me; and Dick as well as Andy think the same."

"Gee whiz! the lost scientists!" burst out the greatly excited and thrilled Phil.

"Looks that way, anyhow," his chum told him. All this time he had never taken his eyes away from that pillar of smoke that was ascending almost perpendicularly toward the sky.

He had a wonderful feeling of jubilation, anxiety, hope, and several other emotions all in a bunch gripping him tight. The ecstacy of that moment, would never fade from his excited memory.

Then something else added to the excitement and strain — the threatening Polar storm! Jim cast a single apprehensive glance toward the south.

Could they beat the storm and effect a rescue in time? He hoped so, with all his heart. How heart-breaking, and provoking it would be if, just when victory seemed within reach something would go wrong.

They were racing ahead now, when every second, counted for so much. Jim again had his eyes glued to his binoculars. The smoke column was plainly discernable now, and alongside stood a curious formation—staring hard Jim immediately concluded it must be some species of domicile formed of cakes of ice welded with half melted snow that had frozen as hard as flint—it looked like a copy of the igloos in which Northern Esquimaux carried on their existence.

Jim was able to note several moving figures, of men. They appeared to be vastly excited, for they were capering about in a most undignified fashion, waving their hands in the air, and probably shouting at the top of their voices, even though Jim of course could not hear this part of the weird performance.

"How does it look for a safe and sane landing?" Dick was booming in the pilot's ear.

Jim saw Andy instantly nod his head—then they were going down on a long slant, heading toward the igloo, at the top of which the observing Jim could now discern a mere shred of the flag formerly waving so gallantly in the wind, to serve as a landmark, should any of the party return to the cache to secure the papers left there by mistake.

"One, two, three!" Dick was now shouting, joyously; "they're all on deck, thank Heaven, and Jules little family will get the wonderful news as soon as we reach Buenos Aires again!"

Two minutes later and the big amphibian touched the smooth surface of the ice field, bumping along for a short distance, and finally coming to a stop within a dozen yards of where that little party of exiles stood awaiting them.

CHAPTER XII

Homeward Bound

Then they were shaking hands with the almost frenzied castaways, who threw their arms tight about each member of the rescue party; and Jim for the first time in his life found himself actually kissed on each cheek of Professor Jules Chapman, who evidently had French blood in his veins.

One of the others, observant Jim quickly noted, amidst the babble of voices, and eager questions concerning the loved ones at home, was limping slightly. Somehow his shrewd mind seemed to grasp what that might signify. Evidently this member of the party had had the misfortune to slip and break a leg even while they were at the lone *cache;* so, too, they must have lost the sledge they drew all the way from the steamer. So it was rendered impossible for them to return, since they would never abandon an injured companion. And here they had lingered for many weeks, their stores gradually dwindled down, and a feeling of daily despair gripping each heart when time passed and they had no news from the balance of the expedition, which for all they knew might have been caught in a terrific ice jam, and crushed with all its crew.

It was a wonderful reunion, and they did not seem as though they could ever get the better of their exuberant spirits.

Dick was the one who remembered something of vast importance—the coming of the storm. He glanced apprehensively toward the south to discover that it had really made alarming progress during the short interval covered by their landing, and that joint celebration with the abandoned trio.

"We've got to get a move on without wasting a minute, Professor," he told his old friend, and comrade on several of the expeditions, results of which had made both of their names famous in all scientific circles.

Of course the three men had noticed the black clouds forging up from the direction of the not so far distant Pole; and they knew only too well what must happen to the big cabin-ship if it caught them on the ice—the furious wind would undoubtedly carry it away as though it were but a chip never to be seen again, when their condition would be rendered even worse than before this happy meeting.

"I must not leave without the precious papers that contain much of the successful surveys we made—they were left here through a grievous mistake, and our hike was simply to save them. Just a fraction of a minute, Dick, my dear friend, and I will join you."

That was all that was necessary—all further particulars could be held back until a more propitious opportunity came for the interesting recital. He vanished inside the ice igloo, while the others made frantic haste to climb aboard the amphibian. Andy tried to see if things were favorable straight ahead, for the runway preceding the ascent; and felt sure it, was as he termed it, "okey." But then no other course was open to them anyways, there being no gap in the ice fields that they could see, to be utilized for gaining the necessary speed and lifting power to start an ascent.

Hardly had the last one climbed aboard when Professor Jules came hurriedly out of the igloo, clutching a handful of papers which he must have just snatched up in great haste.

Dick and Jim were waiting to assist him into the cabin by catching both his arms and lifting; so the very last of the party came aboard in great style. Even then the motors had commenced humming madly as if eager to make the break, and soar through the ether as the natural element of an airship.

Now they were off, gradually gaining more and more momentum, with considerable rough bumping that made their teeth rattle, and their hands grip the nearest stable object lest they drop to their knees.

Jim saw that it was high time they were leaving the ice field, which would soon be in the grip of a furious gale. He held his breath a few seconds when he knew Andy was about to put things to a test—but the boat rose like a lark, and commenced climbing as if in a race for a prize. That indeed was just what it meant, the trophy for which they competed being their own precious lives. It was absolutely necessary that they get above that mass of coming clouds before the fury of the gale burst upon them, and sent them into a fatal tail spin.

Fortunately they were fleeing from the storm, at the rate of two miles each and every minute; and the pilot at the helm was a veteran at his job, so several things were in their favor.

Never would Phil be apt to forget that brief period when it seemed as if the race was nip-and-tuck, now in, and now out. He stared aghast at that turbulent mass of inky clouds that looked so terrible one could easily believe the end of the world was at hand.

Even above the racket aboard the amphibian Phil was certain he could catch the greater din made by the winds accompanying the onward rush of that gale. From that hour on he would know to a certainty what a Polar storm really meant, and feel a subdued species of respect for the same.

But fortune was again kind to them, and they managed to gain their goal before the wind could seize them in its deadly grip, to hurl them down to the moving ice-pack lifeless.

Still Andy kept on climbing; the further they put the clouds and winds in their rear the better, he believed, and Andy ought to know if anybody did, what a close shave they had passed through.

Phil could hardly take his admiring eyes off Professor Jules, smiling face; to the admiring boy the noted man of science was indeed a great hero, at whose shrine he would fain worship. But on the part of the other doubtless his every thought was centered on the beloved little family Dick was now telling him about, and whose anxiety would soon be eased when they reached the region of radio transmission, also international telegraph and telephone lines.

Later on when a fitting chance presented itself the rescuing party sat around and listened while Professor Chapman told the interesting story of their exile at the *cache*.

As he drank in every word Jim realized that he had made a wonderfully close guess in trying to figure things out before they landed to meet those valiant souls who had stuck it out with true American courage and pertinacity.

The sledge had been lost in a dramatic way when they were crossing a crevasse, where the ice was dividing, and they had a narrow escape from being separated one from another. And the stout scientist, Professor Donald Parsons, almost as well known as Jules himself *did* break a leg by an unfortunate slip, and a heavy fall.

Still, it was all over now, but the shouting; and after they rejoined those of the *White Bear* the return to Cape Horn would be hastened in every way possible. After that they must head for the Argentine capital, where they could notify those up in the States whose prayers had followed the rescuers over these thousands of miles of mountains, jungles and dreary Polar ice wastes.

Dick had no intention of making the return trip aboard the good old amphibian, which had served their purposes so faithfully; it would be shipped from Buenos Aires by steamer, after they themselves had departed on board an earlier boat. And it would be easy to believe their traveling in this fashion with their hazardous mission fulfilled, was bound to be much more satisfying than the southward air voyage. The great strain that had so frequently weighed their spirits down, and given their dreams a strong touch of uncertainty, was now entirely dissipated, and they were coming back to their native land as more than conquerers, worthy to wear the laurel wreath in spirit, if not reality.

Often Phil sat in his steamer chair, apparently watching the vast waves rising and falling, their tops crested with white manes of foam, but with his thoughts back home. He could never tire of mentally picturing the awe on the well remembered faces of his numerous pals, while they asked all manner of questions, and drank it in with sighs as though envying the wonderful good luck that had first given them a chance to accompany Uncle Dick; and then had so persistently guarded them from any serious bad luck day after day.

And, lest it be forgotten, Dick himself saw to it that Phil's pelt of his white Polar bear, obtained under such thrilling conditions, was properly cured, and fashioned into an attractive rug for his own room at home, where its presence would always bring many delightful events fresh to his mind when he slipped back into his normal groove, with the other members of the patrol to which he and Jim had been so much credit.

THE END.

Read the other books in this same format

THE ETHEL MORTON SERIES

Ethel Morton at Rose House
Ethel Morton's Enterprise
Ethel Morton's Holidays
Ethel Morton at Sweetbrier Lodge

THE CAMPFIRE GIRLS SERIES

The Campfire Girls as Detectives
The Campfire Girls on Caliban Island
The Campfire Girls Flying Around The Globe
The Campfire Girls at Holly House

THE HILLTOP BOYS SERIES

The Hilltop Boys
The Hilltop Boys in Camp
The Hilltop Boys on Lost Island
The Hilltop Boys on The River

THE CLASSIC SERIES

Aesop's Fables
Dicken's Christmas Stories
Helen's Babies
Tom Brown's School Days

THE SCOUT PATROL BOYS SERIES

The Scout Patrol Boys at Circle U Ranch
The Scout Patrol Boys in Yucatan
The Scout Patrol Boys and The Hunting Lodge Mystery
The Scout Patrol Boys in The Frozen South